Bait and Shoot

As Slocum crossed the rocky patch, he heard a moan. His hand flashed to his Colt Navy, but he did not draw. Flopped on his back a dozen yards away stirred a man. He tried to push himself up on his elbows and failed, collapsing back to the ground.

Slocum hurried over.

"You all right? What happened? You get robbed?" The man was short and squat. Not Clem Baransky. But if he had been dry-gulched recently, he might have seen where Baransky went—or where he had been taken.

"Help me. Head. Hurts. Hit me."

Slocum whipped out his pistol and got a shot off at the man on the ground. He recognized him as one of the road agents who had killed Young and Niederman. His bullet went wide, then all hell came crashing down around him . . .

DON'T MISS THESE
ALL-ACTION WESTERN SERIES
FROM THE BERKLEY PUBLISHING GROUP

THE GUNSMITH by J. R. Roberts
Clint Adams was a legend among lawmen, outlaws, and ladies. They called him . . . the Gunsmith.

LONGARM by Tabor Evans
The popular long-running series about Deputy U.S. Marshal Custis Long—his life, his loves, his fight for justice.

SLOCUM by Jake Logan
Today's longest-running action Western. John Slocum rides a deadly trail of hot blood and cold steel.

BUSHWHACKERS by B. J. Lanagan
An action-packed series by the creators of Longarm! The rousing adventures of the most brutal gang of cutthroats ever assembled—Quantrill's Raiders.

DIAMONDBACK by Guy Brewer
Dex Yancey is Diamondback, a Southern gentleman turned con man when his brother cheats him out of the family fortune. Ladies love him. Gamblers hate him. But nobody pulls one over on Dex . . .

WILDGUN by Jack Hanson
The blazing adventures of mountain man Will Barlow—from the creators of Longarm!

TEXAS TRACKER by Tom Calhoun
J.T. Law: the most relentless—and dangerous—manhunter in all Texas. Where sheriffs and posses fail, he's the best man to bring in the most vicious outlaws—for a price.

JAKE LOGAN

SLOCUM
ON THE
SCAVENGER TRAIL

JOVE BOOKS, NEW YORK

THE BERKLEY PUBLISHING GROUP
Published by the Penguin Group
Penguin Group (USA) Inc.
375 Hudson Street, New York, New York 10014, USA
Penguin Group (Canada), 90 Eglinton Avenue East, Suite 700, Toronto, Ontario M4P 2Y3, Canada
(a division of Pearson Penguin Canada Inc.)
Penguin Books Ltd., 80 Strand, London WC2R 0RL, England
Penguin Group Ireland, 25 St. Stephen's Green, Dublin 2, Ireland (a division of Penguin Books Ltd.)
Penguin Group (Australia), 250 Camberwell Road, Camberwell, Victoria 3124, Australia
(a division of Pearson Australia Group Pty. Ltd.)
Penguin Books India Pvt. Ltd., 11 Community Centre, Panchsheel Park, New Delhi—110 017, India
Penguin Group (NZ), 67 Apollo Drive, Rosedale, Auckland 0632, New Zealand
(a division of Pearson New Zealand Ltd.)
Penguin Books (South Africa) (Pty.) Ltd., 24 Sturdee Avenue, Rosebank, Johannesburg 2196,
South Africa

Penguin Books Ltd., Registered Offices: 80 Strand, London WC2R 0RL, England

This is a work of fiction. Names, characters, places, and incidents either are the product of the author's imagination or are used fictitiously, and any resemblance to actual persons, living or dead, business establishments, events, or locales is entirely coincidental.

SLOCUM ON THE SCAVENGER TRAIL

A Jove Book / published by arrangement with the author

PRINTING HISTORY
Jove edition / February 2012

Copyright © 2012 by Penguin Group (USA) Inc.
Cover illustration by Sergio Giovine.

ISBN: 978-0-515-15038-4

JOVE®
Jove Books are published by The Berkley Publishing Group,
a division of Penguin Group (USA) Inc.,
375 Hudson Street, New York, New York 10014.
JOVE® is a registered trademark of Penguin Group (USA) Inc.
The "J" design is a trademark of Penguin Group (USA) Inc.

PRINTED IN THE UNITED STATES OF AMERICA

10 9 8 7 6 5 4 3 2 1

1

"Price don't matter. Outta my way and lemme buy it!"

John Slocum looked at the wild-eyed prospector and then at his poke brimming with silver coins. There might even be a gold eagle or two in Harry Hawkins's leather pouch that would set as well in Slocum's pocket as that of the merchant.

Slocum interposed himself between the clerk and the prospector, but the merchant wasn't having any of it.

"Out of his way, mister. Let him see how fine my merchandise is. Why, a man could get rich with a pick and shovel this good. You don't want to keep him from getting *rich*, do you?"

Slocum saw the greed on the prospector's face and knew the pitch had worked. Hawkins fumbled out the exorbitant price, ready to pay for a used pick and shovel with a bent blade.

"Somebody's carved their initials in the handle of the pick," Slocum pointed out.

"Don't matter."

"Does," Slocum insisted. "That's bad luck using another man's tools. Swing that pick once and the handle might break."

1

"What's your interest in telling this fine gentleman such lies?" The clerk puffed out his chest and strained the tie on his apron as his potbelly bulged. That might work for alley cats and prairie hens intent on intimidating their foes, but Slocum wasn't having any part of such posturing.

"He's hired me to see him to the gold claims—and out-fitted proper-like," Slocum replied, then he said to Harry, "Why don't you ask how he happened to have this used equipment with the initials *RK* scratched in the handle?"

The clerk moved his bulk around a bit more to position himself between Slocum and his client at the question.

"What's that supposed to mean?" asked Hawkins. His bloodshot eyes went wide as he raked at his beard with dirty fingers. He stepped a few inches closer to see what the clerk offered. For two cents, Slocum would have walked away, but he knew Hawkins had more money than good sense. For what he had offered Slocum to guide him over the pass, a man could live well for a month. And Slocum intended to do just that—if Hawkins didn't squander his entire poke because the merchant found the right sockdolager that appealed to both greed and the golden dream of all pro-spectors.

"Glad you inquired. This here pick belonged to the lucki-est varmint what ever set foot on the Desolation Mountain trail. He used this pick—this very one—to strike it so rich he don't have call to swing it himself anymore. He's got a hundred men working in that mine for him."

"RK?"

"Richard, uh, King," the merchant said. "Everyone's heard of him. Ask around town who's the richest son of a bitch to ever stake a claim, and they'll all say Richard King."

"So the town assayer would know him?" Slocum asked. "And the land office would have a record of where his claim got staked?" He moved around and got a shoulder back in front of the prospector. "Might be useful knowing where this huge strike was so you can start prospecting around there."

"Oh, King's got it all sewed up. You have to go farther into the hills, beyond Desolation Pass now. That's where all of them are going." The clerk swept his arm around, snaked it behind the prospector's back, and turned him to see the muddy streets filled with teams of mules and men getting themselves ready for the arduous climb up the side of the damnedest, most dangerous mountain in all of Idaho.

"We gotta hurry, Slocum. We gotta. All them fellas are gonna get to the gold first."

"Twenty dollars for a pick is twice what you ought to pay." Even at this, Slocum knew the merchant was criminally overcharging, but the equipment and all the other necessary supplies had to be freighted into the town of Almost There over treacherous roads hardly wider than a wagon. That added cost to everything.

"I ain't no crook," the merchant said, all puffed up and looking hurt. "I'll throw in a chisel for nothing. You need a chisel to work the real hard rock." He grabbed a short piece of iron and thrust it into Hawkins's trembling hands.

"That's just a piece of railroad track you've sharpened," Slocum said.

"Means you got a piece of damn good iron. Them rails hold the country together and bring prosperity to us all. That makes this here chisel patriotic—and lucky for whoever uses it."

"I don't want them other men gettin' the jump on me, Slocum," Hawkins said. "Here. And the shovel and chisel, too." He thrust out the money as if it would burn a hole in his hands.

Slocum knew this might be the most money Hawkins would ever see again since the bulk of the prospectors rushing up the mountain pell-mell weren't successful. From what he heard about getting over Desolation Pass, Hawkins might not live long enough to be a failure at prospecting.

"I can fix you up with dynamite, if you've a mind." The clerk made the prospector's money disappear faster than honey off a brown bear's nose. "Mighty hard rock up in the mountains and blasting gets you to the mother lode fast."

"You know anything about blasting?" Slocum asked. He saw the blank look Hawkins gave and knew the answer. "You can blow yourself up mighty easy if you don't have the experience."

"I can give him all he needs to know in a few words, mister," the clerk said. "Why, I see men come and go all the time and know a real smart, lucky one when I see him. Your friend's gonna be so rich he can buy the whole damn town 'fore you know it. We won't call it Almost There. It'll have to be renamed Mighty Rich." The clerk pulled Hawkins closer and said confidentially, "You're gonna be so rich you can buy and sell Robert King a dozen times over."

"You said his name was Richard," Slocum needlessly pointed out.

"Robert's his younger brother. Even more successful than Richard."

Slocum stopped arguing and let Hawkins spend his money. The equipment was used and wouldn't stand up to real work, but Slocum had seen Hawkins's type before. The lure of sudden wealth blinded him to the hard work it took to actually get rich mining. Even if a prospector hit gold, most sold the claim for a song and dance because the hunt was more important than the blue dirt. Those that actually proved their claims put in eighteen hours a day of backbreaking work and seldom did better than a merchant in town.

Slocum snorted. If he was any judge, the only one getting rich off this gold rush was the clerk convincing Hawkins he could use the dynamite safely to uncover an entire mountain of solid gold.

Slocum stepped out into the muddy street and sank up to his ankles. Turning, he looked up at Desolation Mountain and shook his head. The imposing peak was steep, sheer, a widow maker made from solid rock. The clouds swirling around the top might have been an angel's halo but their lead gray underbelly promised something closer to hell for anybody caught on the slopes. A moment of doubt fluttered through his mind when he considered the chore ahead of him. He wasn't afraid of the mountain. He might not have gone through the high pass before, but he had survived considerable danger and woe in his life. Desolation Mountain would be a challenge but one he could win.

The snow-capped peak disappeared as he turned his eyes down the main street of Almost There. Boomtowns came and went, sometimes in days, and this one wasn't going to be different. The news of the gold strike had spread fast, pulling con men like the merchant still busily selling Harry Hawkins equipment he didn't need. Slocum wanted to point out that Hawkins had to carry every pound of it up the mountain slope but held his tongue. The greenhorn would shed his worthless equipment pound by pound as the going got harder.

"We 'bout ready, Mr. Slocum?"

He turned and saw the other three in the party. Clement Baransky spoke for the others with some authority. Slocum had never asked but thought Baransky might have been a lawyer or politician of some sort before getting bitten by the gold bug. From the look of his hands, he wasn't a farmer or any profession requiring hard work. In spite of this, Slocum thought Baransky of all the men paying him a hundred dollars apiece was most likely to find his pot of gold. He wasn't the kind who ever quit, and he hinted at knowledge of rocks and gold the others lacked.

The other two, Young and Niederman, never stopped yapping about what they were going to spend their money on when they struck it rich. Niederman looked to be a farrier from the size of his forearms and the power in his hands. Telltale burns on his face and fingers told of molten metal spatters. While he might have been hit by shrapnel during the war, he didn't look old enough to have seen the horrors Slocum had.

Young was just that, young. Hardly eighteen, he was likely the son who wasn't going to inherit his papa's farm and had to venture out to make his own fortune. The few stories Young had related around the campfire told of a big family, but he had never come right out and said where he fit in among the three sisters and two other brothers.

"Still time to back out," Slocum told Baransky. He watched the man's thin lips curl slightly into a hint of a smile.

"Always time to back out, but I want to go on."

"You're wrong," Slocum said. "There might not be any way to stop once we get going. It's spring but the altitude makes for nasty snowstorms year 'round."

"I see the snow up there," Baransky said, nodding. "I've got a heavy coat and decent wool socks."

Slocum laughed, then called to Hawkins to get his ass in gear. The man struggled with the box of dynamite, the pick, the shovel, and other equipment sold him by the clerk, who'd grinned from ear to ear at a job well done. Hawkins had hardly stepped into the mud when the merchant moved in on another prospector to sell more of his used equipment.

"Give me a hand, will you? I can't carry all this." Hawkins almost dropped the crate of dynamite. Only Slocum's quick reflexes saved it from landing in the mud.

"You get the fuse with this? And blasting caps?" He looked into the crate and saw a few feet of waxy black miner's fuse but nothing else save for the dynamite.

"Blasting caps? What's that?"

Slocum shoved the box back into Hawkins's arms, causing the man to stumble and go to one knee in the mud.

"You'll find out when you try to set off a stick or two," he said. Without another word, he slogged through the mud, heading for the edge of town, where they had camped. Behind him he heard Baransky explaining how dynamite needed the volatile blasting cap to detonate, that the fuse didn't set off the dynamite directly but rather the cap, which then set off the dynamite. Hawkins grumbled about being rooked, then started in on how Slocum should have given him better advice.

Baransky was soon walking alongside Slocum.

"You tried to stop him from buying all that," the tall, whipcord-thin man said. "I heard."

"You always so attentive?"

"I didn't mean to eavesdrop," Baransky said hurriedly. "It's just that I'm a greenhorn, at least when it comes to gold prospecting. I want to learn as much as I can, and you sound like a man with considerable experience." His eyes dropped to the worn ebony handle of the Colt Navy thrust into Slocum's cross-draw holster.

"Good way not to make the same mistakes," Slocum allowed.

"They talk a good game and they look the part, I suppose, but none of them really knows what they're doing, do they? None of us do." This rueful admission caused Slocum to look at Baransky.

"Then why the hell are you risking your life searching for a will-o'-the-wisp? You're an educated man."

"Nothing gets past you, does it?"

"More 'n I can say for you. Those three know nothing about prospecting. If I had to bet on it, you'd be the one with my money on his name to strike it rich."

"Why's that?"

"You take the time to think things through. You're not impulsive like them. Might be greed is gnawing at your guts, too, but you hide it better. And I don't see you quitting when your first bite off the mountain doesn't glitter with a solid gold nugget."

"It's a good thing I don't play poker," Baransky said. "You'd clean me out real quick."

"For a while I might come out ahead. Reckon you would learn fast to gamble just like you're going to learn to prospect for gold."

Baransky laughed and smiled almost shyly.

"You make me think I might actually succeed."

Slocum started to ask what drove the man, who otherwise sounded sensible, to pursue such a dream. Hawkins interrupted him.

Huffing and puffing, Hawkins demanded, "When we gettin' outta here? There's still light."

"Yeah, we need to get on the trail." Young looked around anxiously at the other parties forming.

From what Slocum could tell, no one else was within a day of starting the long uphill trek. Most needed to buy supplies, get water, and find pack animals. He had taken care of those details for his small knot of prospectors already.

"If you're game, we can put a few miles behind us before sundown."

They were.

After they started up the trail, Slocum began to think he should give back the money and let them go on by themselves. Their constant chattering like magpies disturbed the quiet, but more than this, their boasts about striking it big and what they'd do with the money galled him. All except Clem Baransky. He kept his head down and silently plodded along, conserving his strength because he of was the only one of the lot who had seen how steep the road turned in a very short time.

The grade increased and even the surefooted pack mules Slocum had purchased began to strain. More than this, Slocum felt his lungs begin to burn as if he sucked in cheap whiskey with every breath. The altitude robbed him of air. The only good result came with boastful words replaced by harsh breathing.

"Let's camp here for the night," Slocum said, finding a clearing with a small pond of sweet water in the center. From the debris and sooty fire pits, more than one expedition had also used this site.

"We kin go on. Another couple miles." Hawkins gasped out the words. His face was redder than a beet and he might explode at any instant. But he wanted to press on.

"We camp here."

"We only been walking a few hours. How long 'til we make the pass?" Hawkins grasped the pack on the nearest mule for support. The animal turned, ready to kick out. Hawkins sensed what was happening and transferred his weight to a gnarled oak. Even this bent slightly under the load he placed on it.

"There's no reward for getting to the pass first," Slocum said.

"There is, too!" Hawkins shot bolt upright. "If any of those thieves in town reach the goldfields 'fore us, they'll steal our gold. *My* gold!"

"T'ain't yer gold, 'less you find it," said Niederman. "But you got a point. We get there first, we kin find the best places to hunt."

Slocum let them argue among themselves as he began setting up camp. He was spending the night here. The climb had been only a thousand feet but it felt as if it were miles because of the steep grade.

"Gentlemen," said Baransky, "we're not the first up there, so the easiest claims have been made. No matter when we reach the goldfields, we are going to have a real search ahead of us. A day or two isn't going to matter."

"Yeah," Slocum said, dropping a pack to the ground. "Richard King already hit the biggest strike."

"King? Who's that?" asked Young.

Niederman and Baransky turned when Hawkins cleared his throat, then pulled out the pick with the *RK* initials cut into the handle. Slocum half listened as Hawkins regaled them with the bogus tale of the king of the gold mines as he laid a fire and got coffee brewing.

He looked up when Baransky came over.

"I can do some of the cooking. Learned when I was on the trail," the man said.

"Not going to argue. My cooking's so bad even the coyotes puke it up."

"Doubt that," Baransky said. He began opening a pack and working on fixing a mess of beans.

"Why are you risking your life?" Slocum asked. "You don't look the type. Not like them." He jerked his thumb in the direction of the other three, still playing one-upmanship as to who'd find the most gold. None of them considered they might all fail to strike it rich.

"I have my reasons." Baransky got a far-off look and fell silent. Slocum had seen this before. Some men played it close to the vest. Whatever brought Clem Baransky out here was going to stay his own business. He could respect that since he didn't cotton much to anyone prying into his affairs.

The beans were edible and the coffee washed them down. A can of peaches each completed the meal.

"When we headin' out, Slocum?" Young asked. "I got a feelin' we're in a race. Them others, the ones in town, they all had a haunted look to 'em. Hollow eyes and flushed cheeks and they all looked like they'd been in a race just to get to Almost There."

"Reckon who's the hungriest to be rich wins," Slocum said. "We'll be out of here at sunrise."

He tethered the mules and then prowled the perimeter to be sure nothing was creeping up on them. He didn't worry about bears, not yet since they were just stirring from hibernation, but coyotes and wolves and maybe even cougars this close to town became scavengers living off what scraps men carelessly left behind.

After making his rounds, he found all four men sound asleep and sawing wood. Their snores echoed loud enough to keep away any animal. Slocum spread out his own bedroll and lay staring at the stars for a while. The others were already exhausted. The going would get worse. In a few minutes he, too, drifted to sleep.

When he awoke in the morning, he sat up and looked around uneasily. It took a few seconds to figure out what was wrong. Harry Hawkins was gone.

2

"Anybody see what happened to him?" Slocum stood, stretched, and then began a slow circuit of the camp to read the signs in the dirt. The others all denied knowing anything, and he believed them. From all he could tell, Hawkins had left just before dawn. One deep cut in the grass left by his boot heel showed condensation that wouldn't have been present if he had snuck from camp later.

"Maybe he was kidnapped," suggested Niederman.

Slocum shook his head. He found only Hawkins's tracks.

"If road agents had come to rob us, they would have taken all our mules. Only one's missing."

"A good point, Mr. Slocum." Baransky followed him as he pieced together Hawkins's last minutes in the camp, learning what signs were important and which weren't.

His presence annoyed Slocum, but he said nothing. The man didn't get in his way, and the more he learned about tracking now, the easier it would be for them all higher on the mountainside.

"Then why'd he go if he ain't been kidnapped?" Young scratched himself as he spoke.

"Dummy," said Niederman. "He lit out to get ahead of us, that's what happened. He's gonna beat us to the gold! Ain't I right, Slocum?"

"Looks about right to me."

"Why'd he go and do a fool thing like that? In the dark and all alone?"

"Because he doesn't know what he's getting into," Slocum said. There was nothing but trouble ahead for Hawkins trying to make it on his own. Their first day on the trail had been easy compared to the steep climb ahead.

"That man don't have the sense God gave a goose." Young scratched himself some more, hinting at crabs dining on his flesh. "What's fer breakfast?"

"Chow down," Slocum said. "I'll find him to be sure he's all right."

"Do you think he's in danger?"

Slocum looked at Baransky and shrugged. When a man like Hawkins took it into his head that even his traveling companions were out to steal his gold, there was no telling what trouble he could get into.

"You want me to come along?"

"No need. I don't think I'll be gone all that long, one way or the other."

Baransky stiffened when he realized what Slocum meant. Either Hawkins would be brought into the fold or he was gone, maybe dead, maybe rushing headlong up the mountain to find his fortune.

Slocum began the arduous task of hiking up the road. He had asked in town and decided that horses were out of the question for this climb. The road, such as it was, amounted to little more than a rocky path in places, and what they had already traversed was the best traveled and easiest. The steepness made riding impossible. Why lead a horse the entire way rather than riding it? Slocum saw no reason. On the lower levels such as the one he trudged up now, a horse with rider could make better time, but a day farther up the mountain that would change. Even mules would be challenged by the precipitous climb.

Slocum kept his eye on the rocky path and saw plenty of signs that Hawkins had come this way. When he came to a branch, he stopped and frowned at what he saw. For whatever reason, Hawkins had not continued directly up the trail to the pass but had taken the fork to the left.

A quick look ahead caused Slocum to guess that Hawkins had been cowed by the narrow passage between the rocks. He might even have tried to get through and had his mule balk. Unaccustomed to working with pack animals, he had thought the fork edging off at a gentle slope was a better way to go, an easier route to riches.

Grumbling, after more than an hour and not overtaking the prospector, he began to worry. Unless Hawkins had left camp far earlier than he had thought and showed more stamina than he had the day before on the relatively easy climb, something was wrong. Bad wrong.

Replaying all he had seen at the fork convinced Slocum he was on Hawkins's trail. The scratches on the stone, the lack of evidence of new tracks beyond the rocky passage on the main trail, and other small things had built up to convince Slocum he wasn't wrong thinking the prospector had come this way.

He rounded a bend and caught his breath. His hand went to his six-shooter but he didn't draw. Caught in a patch of prickly pear cactus, Hawkins's broad-brimmed hat stirred fitfully in a cool, gentle spring breeze. Slocum yanked the hat free. Hawkins would never abandon it, even if a gust of wind had taken it from his head and dropped it among the spiny cactus pads.

Pulling the embedded spines out would take a few minutes, but the protection offered by the hat, its usefulness as a bucket and as a shield for the face, and all the other reasons a man wore a hat would be apparent even to a greenhorn like Hawkins.

Slocum dropped to his knees and began going over the ground. Dried blood along the trail caught his eye. He scraped some off with his fingernail but couldn't tell how long it had been on the small stone. Wind and water might wash it away but that could take an entire season. Nothing told him this was human blood, much less Hawkins's.

However, in his gut he knew it was. Something bad had happened to the prospector.

Stride long now, he came to a steep downward slope in the trail. At the bottom Hawkins lay sprawled facedown. Even at this distance Slocum saw he was dead.

More than this, he saw that his body had been stripped.

Skidding down the slope with tiny, loose pebbles making his descent all the more treacherous, he came to a halt beside the man's body. His boots had been pulled off, revealing wool socks with big holes in them. Hawkins still wore his pants and a shirt but his coat and vest had been removed. Using the toe of his boot, Slocum rolled the body over. Hawkins flopped flat on his back and revealed a tiny spot of blood.

Someone had walked up, shoved a pistol into his chest, and fired. The powder burn showed that, along with some small singeing of the cloth. The small dot of blood told Slocum that the prospector had died almost instantly. He had seen this in battle too many times. Sudden death prevented more than a drop or two from being pumped out of the body. The killing shot had gone straight through Hawkins's heart and exited his back.

He looked around, hand resting on his six-shooter, but saw nothing. Whoever had killed Hawkins had gone back along the trail in the direction he had been heading. Slocum had no desire to bring the killer and thief to justice. The prospector had been stupid leaving the group and ignorant in the ways of getting his mule through the rocky gap along the actual trail.

"The mule," muttered Slocum. The killer had taken not

only the mule but all the supplies on it. Somehow the loss of the pack animal and all it carried bothered him more than Hawkins's death.

Burying the man was out of the question in the rocky ground. Even if he had been Hawkins's best friend, carrying the body back would also have been out of the question. The trail was too steep and the going too difficult before he could find a level stretch where a decent grave could be dug.

He could have used some of the dynamite Hawkins had bought to blast a grave, but that had been stolen, too.

Slocum cast one last look at Hawkins. Insects already worked on his flesh. It wouldn't be long before the buzzards and even coyotes came in to finish off their meal. Turning his back on the corpse, he drove his toes into the steep slope and made his way back up the trail. It took less time to return than it had to find Hawkins because he wasn't slowed by studying the rocky ground for spoor.

But he ought to have been more alert. He reached the camp where he had left the other three prospectors and found it empty. Tired, he dropped to a rock and heaved a sigh of frustration.

He had collected half his fee from each man, so he was two hundred dollars to the good if he simply went back down the mountain. He wasn't ever going to collect the remaining fifty dollars owed him by Harry Hawkins. Was it worth the balance to find what had happened to the trio, who hadn't bothered following his advice to stay here?

It didn't matter. He heaved himself to his feet. Money wasn't at the heart of his decision. He had hired on to do a job and couldn't turn his back on it. Some small guilt gnawed at him because he should have recognized the gold fever in Hawkins and the chance he would do something stupid.

Hawkins couldn't have been stupider. He took the wrong path and got himself gunned down by road agents. As Slocum trudged back up the trail he had already traversed twice that day, he wondered how prevalent such thievery was. The prospective gold miners were flush with equipment and some even had a few greenbacks tucked into their pocket after escaping the avaricious merchants down in Almost There. Mules and other, heavier equipment would fetch a good price back at the base of the mountain.

A frown wrinkled his forehead as he wondered if the pick Hawkins had bought—the one with another man's initials carved in it—had been lost in the same way. A lucrative trade could be built up if you were unscrupulous enough. A few men on the mountain trail killed the prospectors, stole their equipment, and sold it to the merchants in town, who resold it at ever higher prices to new prospectors.

He couldn't prove it, but he didn't care. He wasn't a lawman and had no call to do their job. A man had to rely on himself. Slocum snorted at the thought. If a man couldn't do a chore, he hired someone to help him.

Slocum walked faster. He had been hired to guide Baransky, Young, and Niederman to the goldfields on the other side of Desolation Pass. Because they had lit out didn't mean squat. He had to do his job.

As he walked, he saw more evidence of the trio along the trail that he had missed before. He came to the fork where Hawkins had gone wrong. The three with their mules had shown more determination and had pushed through the narrow passage. Ample signs on the far side of the tight passage proved it. When he found fresh mule flop, he knew they had come this way.

For another twenty minutes, the steep trail sapped his energy but then it leveled out. Trees clustered ahead and to both sides, hinting at water. His mouth felt like the inside of a cotton bale. He kept walking, eyes on the trail, until he came to another fork. One prospector had continued into thick woods. Dropping to his belly, Slocum stared parallel to the ground to better eye the tracks as they went across grassier terrain.

"One went on by himself, two others headed for the

trees." He suspected the men choosing the forested area were the smart ones. They could find water and a place to gather firewood to prepare a hot meal. The one pressing on might end up like Hawkins.

Hiking alone in such rugged territory was foolhardy.

Slocum started after the solitary prospector but hadn't gone ten paces when gunfire sounded from off to his left—in the direction taken by the two prospectors.

A million ideas about what happened flashed through his mind. There might have been a falling-out between the two. He decided that wasn't too likely. Any gunplay would happen over nuggets and claims. They were hardly a day into their trek across Desolation Mountain.

More gunfire caused him to turn from the path leading higher into the hills and toward the copse. He identified three different reports. Even if the two men had decided to shoot it out, they would have used only two weapons. A third distinctive gunshot brought back his concern over road agents killing and robbing those on the mountainside.

Before he reached the edge of the trees, he heard another pistol fire. It might have been a black powder gun from the muffled sound reaching through the forest. The answering fusillade made him cringe. One side tried to throw enough lead to cover an attack. He pictured it in his mind. The two prospectors fearfully used their own old, rusty six-shooters as they were attacked by determined outlaws.

Slocum slid the Colt from his holster and advanced cautiously. To burst out into the middle of the gunfight was worse than foolish—it would be suicidal. Both sides would open up on him. He had to find what was happening and then choose his tactics carefully.

A bullet sang past his head, forcing him to a crouch behind a tree. He peered around the bole of the juniper and tried to make out where the gunman ahead of him lay in wait. It took a full minute to realize no one had targeted him; the bullet was a stray slug from the increasingly noisy fight ahead.

Remaining in a crouch, he advanced, every sense alert. Another slug ripped away a splinter above him, forcing him to the ground. As he flattened out, he saw Niederman's back not ten yards away. The prospector wasn't moving. Slocum began wiggling forward until he caught Young's attention. The man's eyes were wide with fear. He clutched an old Griswold & Gunnison .36 in one hand. Slocum hadn't seen one of those pistols since the war. Young might well have been given it as part of his inheritance from a father or older brother. In his other hand he held a Colt Dragoon.

"Slocum!" Young half turned. "Help me. Niederman's dead. They shot him!" He held up the Colt and stared at it. "I took this from him, but I'm out of ammo."

A bullet whined past the man's ear, making his eyes go even wider in fear. He sat down fast to get out of sight.

"What happened?"

"I dunno. They snuck up and started shooting. Never gave us no warning or anything!"

"Why'd you leave camp when I told you to stay?" Slocum sat beside Young, pried the Colt from the man's hand, and saw that it was empty. Hunting for ammo on the dead Niederman or locating his gear and finding a box of cartridges was out of the question. A new barrage tore at the trees all around, sending splinters and sap flying in all directions.

"No reason to wait. There's gold a'waitin' us up there."

"All you're going to find is a grave," Slocum said. He chanced a quick look around and knew his worst fear had been realized. The sudden increase in lead filling the air meant at least one road agent was intent on keeping them pinned down while another—others—circled to get behind.

"They're sneaking up on us, probably coming from both flanks," Slocum said. "You got more ammunition for that old gun?"

Young lifted the G&G and stared at it as if he had never seen it before in his life.

"Reload and try not to get your head blown off."

"Wait, Slocum, you can't go. You—" Young gasped as a bullet ripped through his shoulder, sending a red spray out into Slocum's face.

He shoved Young back. The man gasped in pain.

"They shot me!"

"They're going to kill you like they did Niederman unless you fight. Don't give up. Try to surrender and they'll cut you down where you stand."

Young's mouth opened like he was a fish washed up on a riverbank. No words came out. Slocum saw that he had read the man's mind perfectly. It sounded safe to Young to give up. Drop his pistol, throw up his hands, the outlaws wouldn't shoot at him anymore.

"You understand? They're not going to leave any of us alive. They are going to kill you and steal everything you have."

"I . . . I'll give it to them! They don't have to shoot me again!"

Slocum reached out and drove strong fingers into the shoulder wound. Young screeched in pain.

"Why're you hurtin' me, Slocum?"

"To force some sense into your head." He squeezed again and forced Young to thrash about and pull away from him. "It'll hurt a whole lot worse if you surrender."

Young nodded once, turned, and rested his old six-shooter on the top of the rock where he crouched and squeezed off a shot.

It went high, but Slocum didn't care if Young was a marksman. Flinging lead kept the outlaws honest—a little.

He left Young and went into the woods to intercept whoever tried to sneak up from behind. Only a dozen yards into the woods, he saw a man dressed like a miner in canvas pants and a black-and-red-checked shirt moving in fast. He carried a sawed-off shotgun like he knew how to use it.

Slocum took careful aim and fired, then cursed. His bullet had struck a twig and deflected just enough to prevent a killing shot. The outlaw yelped and fell forward but wasn't permanently out of the fight.

Or out at all.

Knowing he had no time left to lay another ambush, Slocum pushed forward with reckless abandon. He made as much noise as he could as he yelled, whooped, and hollered.

"Charge, boys, get 'em. There's only the one! We got 'im outnumbered!"

He didn't care if the outlaw believed his shouted lies. All he wanted was a moment of hesitation. And he got it.

The outlaw came to his knees and looked around. As he looked into the woods to his right, Slocum came on from his left. Another shot broke the man's wrist. Then Slocum swung his Colt Navy as hard as he could. The barrel crunched into bone. The outlaw keeled over, out like a light.

Slocum scooped up the shotgun and waited to see if the felled outlaw had a partner.

He heard nothing but the sporadic shooting from behind him. Then came another flurry of gunfire.

And then nothing. The silence was so great that it hurt Slocum's ears.

Finally an unfamiliar voice crowed, "Got the son of a bitch. Blowed his fool head right off. Let's get his gear and clear out."

Slocum clutched the shotgun, wondering what he ought to do. Then it was decided for him.

3

"Where's Weasel?"

"He was goin' 'round to come up from behind," said a second outlaw.

Slocum flinched when a third voice rang through the forest.

"Weasel! Git yer ass over here right now. We got work to do. Don't want you out there communin' with nature."

Three men laughed uproariously, warning Slocum that they'd hunt for their partner when the joke wore off. They'd come out mad at him, or maybe they were crafty enough to think he had run afoul of someone with Young. He backed away, careful to keep from making much noise. His palms began to sweat, and the shotgun turned slippery in his grip when he heard them coming.

They moved as silently as he did, no joshing around now. He might get lucky and kill them one by one. More likely, he could drill one of them before the other two closed in on him and shot him as dead as they had Young and Niederman.

He lifted the shotgun, mind racing. His thumb stroked

22

over the hammers, then he moved fast. There wasn't much time, and he doubted it would work, but he had to try something. He knelt beside the man he had buffaloed, grabbed the limp hand, and curled a finger around the trigger. Pulling hard, he raised the body far enough to position the shotgun so the muzzles rested under the man's chin.

He pulled the trigger. The roar was muffled by the outlaw's brains. The top of his head disappeared in a red mist, but Slocum had ducked back to avoid having much spatter him.

"That's Weasel's shotgun," one called to his partners.

Slocum was startled. The voice came from nearby, closer than he'd expected. He started to dart in the other direction, then took the time to move the dead man's boot so the toe tangled up in an exposed tree root. Only then did Slocum crouch and duck walk away from the approaching outlaw.

He barely found shelter behind a rotting log. Stretched out behind it, he hoped the outlaw now standing over the dead body wouldn't notice. Slocum yanked off his hat and crushed it down, then tried to melt into the ground. The side of his face pressed into sticky pine needles, he saw through a hole in the log as the outlaw dropped to one knee and rolled the dead man over.

"The clumsy bastard," the outlaw said, looking up. Two men stepped from shadows to join him. "He tripped and blowed his own damn head off."

"Might be that kid we killed got him?"

"See?" The man who had found Weasel reached down and tried to pull the tangled foot free. Slocum heard bones break as the man jerked hard in his fury and frustration. "He always was clumsier than a drunken rooster peckin' 'round for corn on an outhouse floor. Did him in."

"We got to bury him?"

"Let him rot," the man beside him said, standing.

"More for us. But you think the boss ought to be told what happened?"

"It'll make the boss think we done up and kilt him," said the third man. "I say, we tell the boss he got careless and a prospector got in a lucky shot."

They argued for another minute, finally agreeing that Weasel had been cut down in the heat of battle. They walked away without so much as a backward look—after stripping the body of its weapons, a pocket watch, and a small wad of greenbacks.

Slocum was willing to give them their booty in exchange for getting the hell away alive. He lay behind the log, tense with every sense alert for a hint that they had discovered him. Sounds from the direction of where Niederman and Young had died told him they had the pair's mules. The two dead prospectors were probably stripped of the scant belongings carried on their person, then distant sounds of animals walking away made Slocum hope he was well rid of the killers.

He still remained in hiding for another half hour before standing. Making his way through the woods, he found the bodies of the dead prospectors. His approach scared away a coyote. The snarling animal stood a few yards in front of him, considering how difficult it would be to claim its dinner from a living human.

Slocum didn't want to take the time but felt the obligation. He had taken money from these two for a safe passage across the mountains. Lacking a shovel or any of the other tools that had been stolen, he made a rude grave of stones piled atop the two bodies. Scratching names on a rock using the tip of his knife seemed a poor grave marker, but it was more than the pair would have received if he hadn't come along.

He dropped the marker stone onto the larger pile, then began walking.

It had been a hell of a day. He'd had three of his party murdered and robbed, and he didn't have good feelings the same hadn't happened to Clem Baransky.

* * *

The boomtown was even more crowded than when he had left with his four charges. Slocum didn't draw any attention. Nobody remembered faces. Looking around at the hard cases, maybe some of them took money from eager prospectors and murdered them up on the road across the mountain. Nobody would care if the money got spent in Almost There on booze and hookers.

Slocum dropped into a chair at the back of a long, narrow tent with a crude plank over two sawhorses serving as a bar. A touch of the whiskey on his tongue made him gag. He sucked in a deep breath, then knocked back the shot and let it sear its way to his belly. It might have been the thought of losing all four in the party or it might have been a lack of decent food but the liquor churned and boiled and made him sick to his stomach.

He downed another shot.

This time the alcohol worked to numb him, in both body and mind.

If he drank enough, he might even forget the faces of the men he had signed on to guide.

If he drank more than enough, even the ugly hookers might not look so ugly and would help him forget.

"Sir?"

Slocum looked up but nobody was close to him. A moment's panic seized him as he thought the dead men were speaking to him. Then the voice came again, softer and sweeter than anyone he knew.

"Please, sir, may I speak with you?"

Slocum craned his neck and almost fell from the rickety chair. A woman held up the edge of the tent, staring right at him. For a moment, he thought he recognized her. Then the feeling faded a mite.

"What do you want?"

"A moment of your time, that's all. Please. Can you come outside? Out back of this . . . of this place?"

Slocum took another shot, thinking this desert mirage would go away, but it didn't. She was as pretty as any woman he could remember. Her soft brown hair caught the sun and revealed auburn highlights. Eyes of melted chocolate stared at him from behind impossibly black eyelashes. A hint of rouge gave her cheeks a blush. Or did she use makeup? The rosy color might be natural. Her finely boned cheeks, bow-shaped lips, and strong chin gave Slocum a reason to duck under the tent flap she held for him.

He found himself facing not only the woman but a slender man, perhaps a year or two younger, who was the spitting image of Clem Baransky. Slocum paused as the woman dropped the tent flap and stared at him, as if appraising a prize heifer.

"You will do," she said.

"Pleased to hear that," Slocum said. "Now I'll get back to my drinking."

"One moment!" She reached out and touched his arm, then drew away as if she had touched a hot stove. "My brother and I require your services."

"Gold prospecting is dangerous, too dangerous for the likes of you."

"We have no desire for that," she said. "I am Melissa Baransky and this is Stephen, my brother. We want to hire you to find our father."

Slocum shouldn't have been surprised since the son was the spitting image of his pa, and there were hints of the man reflected in the woman's features.

"I've been doing some thinking on that," he said. Letting Clem Baransky go off on his own was a foolish thing, but losing all four of the men he had been paid to guide to the goldfields was even worse. He knew three were dead but had no idea if Baransky had survived. Getting through Desolation Pass was hard but fighting off road agents intent on stealing equipment and animals added to the threats.

He owed Baransky more than he had delivered.

"I beg your pardon?" Melissa looked at his curiously.

"Why'd you pick me to hunt for him?"

Melissa and her brother exchanged glances again. Slocum noticed that Stephen put his hand in a pocket that already bulged. A small gun hidden there might be fired through the coat. Slocum ignored the motion. These were city slickers and uneasy being surrounded by rough characters. This made him wonder about the Baransky family since Clem had shown himself to possess toughness that wasn't apparent in his children.

"We have asked around and no one else seems . . . likely."

"You mean honest?"

Melissa's lips thinned to a line. She nodded once.

"We know our pa came through only a few days ago, but no one in this town—it doesn't appear to have a name—admits to seeing him." Stephen Baransky looked peeved at this.

"A hundred men a week come through here, maybe more," Slocum said. "And they call the town Almost There, because it's the last town before the gold strike." He could think of other reasons but doubted the Baranskys wanted to hear them.

"You guide them to the goldfields?" Melissa looked at him without guile.

"I just got to town myself," Slocum said, still wondering if they knew he had been hired to guide their pa and were setting him up for an ambush. Even in a wide-open, no-holds-barred boomtown like Almost There, killing in the streets was frowned upon. He hadn't seen a marshal but that didn't mean a vigilance committee couldn't form at the drop of a hat—or the knotting of a noose.

"So you are not skilled enough to do this?"

"Miss, I need equipment. The trail's mighty steep and would require a mule rather than a horse."

"We can afford to outfit you. And . . . and guarantee payment when you return with our father."

"What if I can't?"

"Then you must bring us his body," Melissa said, trying not to cry. She didn't quite make it. A tear glistened at the corner of her eye, but she turned slightly to prevent Slocum from seeing it.

"What's so all-fired important about dragging him away from his prospecting?"

"We—" she began.

"That's none of your business," Stephen said, anger touching his words. A wildness in his eyes banked as suddenly as it appeared. "Will you go after him? For fifty dollars?"

"And the supplies?"

"Yes, yes, of course," Melissa said. "We can place your money in the bank, in escrow."

"No need. I trust you." Slocum smiled grimly. "Don't think there is a bank in town. None of the merchants reckon to stay here long enough."

"But you said a hundred men a week pass through," said Stephen. "I don't understand. Why isn't there a bank?"

"Folks don't trust bankers and rely on their own six-shooters to protect their poke. And a boomtown like this might be a ghost town in a month. A week."

"All the gold will be found so everyone moves on?" Melissa asked.

He wondered if she had any idea how rare it was for any prospector to find enough gold to make the dangerous hunt worthwhile. She acted as if it were a foregone conclusion that every man who reached the goldfields struck it rich.

She shared that notion with her pa and every other man trying to get across the mountains to the Promised Land.

"The real gold's made selling the equipment."

"We know our father departed a few days ago. We were close to reaching him but our wagon broke down and we only recently arrived here." Melissa seemed anxious to explain why they were unable to find their father in time to stop him. Slocum had only passing interest in what was so all-fired important that both brother and sister had to make the effort.

"I don't know how long it'll take," Slocum said. "Might be a few days to find him and that many to return. That's assuming he wants to come back with me."

"Oh, yes, I understand that," Melissa said. "It might be construed that you were attempting, on the behalf of others, to keep him from his goldmine. I have taken care of that." She fished around in a clutch purse and withdrew a small envelope. "This will convince him to return here." She held it out, then pulled it back when Slocum reached for it. "Can you read?"

"Does it matter?"

"The letter is personal. Family business," Stephen said brusquely. "We don't want the information bandied about."

"Who am I going to tell that'd be interested?"

Melissa extended the letter. Slocum tucked it into his coat pocket without even glancing at what was written on the front. He supposed it was her pa's name.

"We'll get you outfitted, if the contract is acceptable to you."

"It's a deal."

"You won't use this opportunity to go hunting for gold on your own, will you?"

"Don't outfit me if you're worried."

"That's no kind of attitude, sir," Melissa said, outraged.

"You either trust me or you don't." He watched emotions play over the woman's lovely face and knew it hardly mattered what she decided. The Baransky family could get him the supplies needed, or not. He was going after her father because he owed it to the man. Abandoning him on the mountainside was nothing short of dereliction of duty.

"Very well," Melissa said. "We will outfit you."

"Melly, please, let's discuss this."

"No, Stephen, we need to move quickly. This gentleman is going to aid us."

"There's one outfitter in town," Slocum said, remembering how the merchant had duped Hawkins. That wasn't going to happen again. "Let me do the dickering."

"We'll see about that," Stephen said coldly.

Brother and sister started toward the merchant's tent, letting Slocum bring up the rear. It was a pointed insult showing that they considered him little more than a servant who could trail behind his betters, but Slocum didn't mind since he got a chance to watch Melissa walk from behind.

"You, sir, a word. We would make a few purchases," Stephen called out. The merchant wiped dirty hands on his equally filthy apron and graced the Baranskys with a broad smile that died when he saw Slocum.

"I need a mule and gear," Slocum said.

"What's happened to—" The merchant bit off his question since it didn't matter. Let Slocum buy everything. Who he sold to was less important than the amount he got for his goods.

"I need a sturdy mule," Slocum said, then detailed the rest of the supplies. A week on the trail would be all he required. Either he found Clem Baransky by then or he didn't and would return to tell his children the man was dead.

"Got a few good ones out back. Let's go take a look at 'em, eh?" The merchant jerked his thumb over his shoulder. Slocum noticed the Baranskys let him lead the way down the muddy alley to the corral out back.

"That's all you have?" Stephen asked.

"Don't need a lot, son, when you got the best. And that's what these are. The best."

Slocum went to the corral and stared at the nearest mule.

"This one's the best you're likely to find," Slocum said.

It was the same mule Clement Baransky had left town riding.

4

"Who sold you the mule?" Slocum asked. He moved along the corral fence to be certain this was Baransky's mule. It was. A peculiar white star off-center on the face was identical, as was a long brown mark on the right front leg.

"Nobody around here has a name. Why should they?"

Slocum glanced at the merchant and knew he was lying.

"Want to buy some more but going straight to the breeder next time will save time and money," Slocum said. He got a short, barking laugh as reply.

"You ain't cuttin' me out no deal, mister. No way. Besides, the gent what sold me these mules ain't a breeder. He just happened to come into them."

"Inherited them," Slocum said in a neutral voice.

"Why aren't we pressing on with this negotiation?" Stephen Baransky glared at Slocum. "Time is of the essence."

"An hour, more or less, isn't going to matter," Slocum said. He walked around the corral, ostensibly to study the other mules. He saw several distinctive boot prints. Someone with a deep V cut in the right heel had walked through the mud recently since the prints hadn't yet disappeared from a welter of mules and other people crowding in.

"I like the youngster's conviction on this. Time's slippin' away fer us all. Strike while the iron's hot."

"I'll take the mule. That one." Slocum pointed to the one Baransky had ridden from town on.

"Now you're talkin'."

"Do we get a bill of sale?"

"Little lady," the merchant said condescendingly, "next thing you'll be wantin' me to sign a paper sayin' I got title free and clear to this animal."

"Don't you?"

The merchant looked at Slocum, then laughed.

"You kin tell her how things're done out here, mister. Either give me one hundred dollars or find another mule."

"Here," Slocum said, peeling off the greenbacks from the roll in his pocket.

"Wait, sir, I said we would—" Melissa started to open her purse, but Slocum grabbed and closed it. He caught the merest flash of a lot of money inside. It wasn't smart flashing that kind of scrip around a boomtown—or any town. How she had survived in the world without getting killed for her money was something of a poser.

"I'll collect that, too, when I get back."

"No, I won't hear of it."

"Let him, Melly. We need to conserve our cash."

"Listen to your brother," Slocum advised her. To the merchant, he said, "I'll be back in an hour. Have all the gear ready for me then."

They dickered a bit more over the price and what was available, then Slocum took both the Baranskys by the arm and steered them away.

"You find a place to stay until I get back in a few days. It might take a week, but if I'm gone longer than that, bet money I'm not coming back at all."

"You mean you will have discovered gold?"

At first Slocum thought the woman was joking, then saw her solemn expression.

"Yeah, that's right."

Stephen Baransky obviously caught Slocum's jest and looked around.

"I need to get some directions first, then I'll be off."

"But," said Melissa, "all you need do is ride up that trail. It is quite well defined and easy to follow. I can tell that from here."

"The trail gets rockier higher up the slope. Getting through Desolation Pass is something of a gamble at the best of times, and spring storms make the way deadly right now."

He tipped his hat to her, exchanged looks with her brother, then headed for the nearest saloon. Stephen made a slighting comment about men who couldn't go without liquor, but Slocum ignored it. He still had a powerful thirst, but whiskey wasn't what he sought. A thief who had just sold a stolen mule would likely wet his whistle before heading back up the mountainside.

And he was likely to head for the nearest gin mill.

Slocum stepped into the saloon and was immediately engulfed in smoke, stale beer odors, and soaring dreams. A half-dozen prospectors pressed against the bar, all talking excitedly about how much gold they would find and what they were going to spend their first million on. He dismissed them out of hand because the owlhoot he sought knew a better way to getting rich.

Three men played cards at a back table and another shot pool at a table propped up with a rock and a few wedges of wood. Slocum moved to the poker table, drawn by the click of chips and soft swishing of cards being dealt, but he turned and stared when the man at the pool table leaned forward to make a difficult across-table shot.

His boot heel was deeply notched in the same way as the print he had discovered at the corral. Slocum dropped into a chair and watched as the man shot and repeatedly missed, then flung the cue onto the table and loudly proclaimed, "Damned table's not level and them balls ain't round neither. How you expect a man to play a proper game with defective equipment?"

"Leastwise the table's got balls. That's more 'n I can say for you," called out the barkeep. "You gonna pay what you owe me or are you gonna just take up space?"

"To hell with you." The man fumbled in his pocket and drew out a thick wad of greenbacks. He peeled off a large number of bills and dropped them on the pool table. "That'll take care of the lot of us."

"You want a bottle of the special to take back with you?"

"Why not? But it had better be real Kaintuck bourbon and not that trade whiskey you boil up. Trueheart ain't gonna put up with it."

"Tell him he's welcome anytime he's in town. You, now, you son of a bitch, clear out."

The two men's animosity boiled over. The pool player went for his six-gun, but the barkeep had a scattergun out and pointed. They stood frozen for a moment, then the man at the pool table stalked out the back door. Slocum shot to his feet and went outside, waiting for the man to come into sight. When he didn't round the building, Slocum went hunting.

Behind the saloon he found only heavy mud that was too deep to take decent tracks. It looked as if the entire 2nd Infantry from Camp Coeur d'Alene had marched across it. Nowhere did he see the man from the saloon. Slocum went back through the rear door and to the bar, where he caught the barkeep's attention.

"I wanted to send a message to Trueheart," he said, "but the gent who was just in here left before I could talk to him."

The barkeep stared at him as if he were made of smoke.

"Don't know nobody named Trueheart," the bartender said. "And you're the only one who's come and gone. What are you drinkin'?"

Slocum left without another word. He was getting hot under the collar but understood what was going on. Trueheart had a gang working the trail leading over the mountains, and everyone in town was beholden to him. The merchant bought and sold stolen equipment many times over and the barkeep made a steady income off profits.

He returned to the corral, where the merchant had dropped a pack and supplies into the mud. Slocum wiped off the filth, carefully packed, making sure he had everything he needed, then lashed the pack down onto the mule's rump. With a jump, he was over and astride the animal, much to its displeasure. It took a few seconds to convince the balky mule he wasn't getting down. With some reluctance, the mule turned of its own accord to the trail leading to Desolation Pass and began walking.

It had been this way before—many times before. Slocum wondered if it had ever gone the entire way.

Going over the same terrain proved easier the second time. Slocum had a good memory for roads he had traveled, and this was no exception. He passed the turnoff where he had insisted the original party camp for the night and pressed on to the rocky gap. Clem Baransky had made it this far. But how much farther along the road had he traveled before being dry-gulched?

Slocum realized he might never find the exact spot—or Baransky's body. It had been pure accident that he had found Hawkins after he had been killed. If the road agents had taken more time and tossed his body over a cliff, the carrion eaters would have reduced Hawkins to skeletal remains within a day or two. The best Slocum could hope was to find where Baransky had been waylaid and maybe bury what was left of him.

He found himself not wanting to upset Melissa Baransky more than necessary. The sight of her pa's half-decomposed body slung over a mule's back would be a shock he could sidestep with a judicious lie. Slocum reached into his coat pocket and drew out the envelope so he could hold it in the fading sunlight. The copper tint the setting sun lent the writing might have been mistaken for blood.

The letter was simply addressed "Father."

What brother and·sister felt was so all-fired important that they had to leave their fancy-ass society and come to Idaho after their pa might be in the letter. Slocum had a passing curiosity about it, but mail was as sacrosanct as a man's word. He would pass it on to Baransky if he found him alive or, more likely, return the unopened letter to Melissa after he gave up hunting for the corpse.

As he swayed along, the surefooted mule hardly missing a step as the road increasingly sloped upward, he found himself almost asleep. The dangers were great and he ought to remain alert, but thoughts of Melissa Baransky kept crowding out attentiveness. She was quite a looker. He reached into his coat pocket and fingered the edge of the envelope, wondering what she had written to her pa and why she had traipsed across the country to this godforsaken edge of nowhere.

It was a mystery but not one Slocum was willing to solve by opening the envelope and reading the letter. Considering how both brother and sister had acted, there might be nothing at all inside. It might be a trick to see how trustworthy he was.

Such thoughts led to ruin. Slocum had no reason to trust them nor did they have any reason to trust him. He was surprised the merchant hadn't mentioned Slocum leading an earlier party out, but chances were good he didn't want to jinx another sale. More than this, Trueheart might not be the only outlaw working the trail. Slocum might have been mistaken for another thief and murderer who could bring immense, immediate wealth to the merchant in return for his silence.

The road reached a plateau and leveled off. Marmots

poked their heads from burrows and watched him warily. Enough prospectors had come past for the small rodents to know they might end up as dinner in a stewpot if they weren't careful. Slocum took the opportunity to look down and see where earlier travelers had gone along this stretch. Most followed the path but enough veered away that he wondered if Baransky had done so only to find himself in an ambush amid a stand of trees. There were still plenty at this altitude. The tree line was another fifteen hundred feet higher on the mountain.

Slocum reared back and looked up at the summit of Desolation Mountain on his right. The saddle pass formed between it and the mountain to the left was at least two thousand feet higher, well above the timberline. It was deceptive, he knew. Two thousand feet was nothing—only this was straight up and his lungs already strained just a mite to suck in air. It would be far worse by the time the pass opened up to spill gold seekers onto the far side of the mountain.

"Where might he have gone?" Slocum asked the mule. The long-eared head turned and a big brown eye fixed on him. Slocum had no better idea, so he dismounted and gave the mule its head. It might go after a tuft of grass or hunt water, but it might also remember the trail it had traversed before with Clem Baransky on its back. Slocum had no better way of tracking.

The mule kicked and tried to free itself of its load. When it realized Slocum had cinched the supplies down too securely, it settled down, turned back to the road, and then started walking at a brisk pace that forced Slocum to lengthen his stride to keep up. He doubted the mule would continue with him on its back, but it seemed content to go along without a rider.

He only hoped this was the same track taken by Baransky.

His hope flared when the mule suddenly veered off the road and went to a small, grassy meadow. It positioned itself near a clump of grass and began eating. Slocum examined the grass and saw it was already half eaten, whether by this mule or some other creature he couldn't tell. But the mule had shown considerable memory before. This might be a safe place for it to eat because it had done so before.

As it grazed, Slocum began circling the area, his search spiral widening until he found footprints. The grass here was crushed as if several men had milled about—or maybe fought. He thought about what he saw and constructed a small stage play of what had happened.

Baransky had let his mule graze, then walked in this direction. A shallow ravine still held spoor where several men had hidden. Or Slocum thought that might be what had happened. Baransky had approached for some reason, then he had been jumped. The scuffle was brief but fierce enough to kick up the thin mountain dirt and grass growing on it.

From here they all headed toward the far side of the meadow.

Slocum lost the tracks because of a rocky patch, but he reckoned that the kidnappers walked straight ahead since Baransky wasn't putting up a fight any longer. Here and there Slocum had found double ruts in the dirt that showed where a man was dragged along facedown, his toes digging into the ground.

As he crossed the rocky patch, he heard a moan. His hand flashed to his Colt Navy, but he did not draw. Flopped on his back a dozen yards away stirred a man. He tried to push himself up on his elbows and failed, to collapse back to the ground.

Slocum hurried over.

"You all right? What happened? You get robbed?" The man was short and squat. Not Clem Baransky. But if he had been dry-gulched recently, he might have seen where Baransky went—or where he had been taken.

"Help me. Head. Hurts. Hit me."

Slocum hurried over, then whipped out his pistol and got

a shot off at the man on the ground. He recognized him as one of the road agents who had killed Young and Niederman. His bullet went wide, then all hell came crashing down around him. From shallow ravines on either side of the road agent boiled three more men, their guns blazing.

Slocum felt an instant of sharp pain, threw up his hands, and knew his six-shooter went flying through the air. Then the world turned black, and he knew nothing more.

5

Flies buzzing. Hot sun burning his face. Slocum moaned and tried to bat both away. The fly might have been scared off by his feeble swatting but the sun still cooked his flesh. He dropped his hand to shield his eyes and slowly opened them. Sun filtered through his fingers. For a few seconds, it annoyed him, then he realized what it meant and he rejoiced.

He was still alive.

Trying to roll onto his side proved harder than it should have. Tightness along the side of his head turned to utter pain when he moved. He stopped screening his eyes and traced the long, narrow crease left by a bullet. The pain he caused pressing into the wound focused him and brought everything rushing back.

Ignoring the discomfort, he sat up and squinted hard to keep his eyes in focus. He lay in the grassy field where he had thought to be a Good Samaritan and rescue another victim of the scavengers. Instead, he had fallen prey to them.

"That's how they got Baransky," he said. His voice was raspy, hoarse, his lips chapped and feeling like old dried-out rubber. "One decoyed him close and the others grabbed

40

him." Slocum tried to stand but wasn't up to it yet. He sat heavily, regaining his strength. "Why'd they kidnap him and not kill him on the spot?"

The answer trickled through the barricades that pain threw up in his brain. They had thought he was dead. The dried blood on his head and face made it look as if they had blown his brains out.

Every instant of the brief gunfight rushed back. He reached across to his holster. Empty. Swinging around, he hunted for his Colt and found it twenty feet away. When he had been shot, he had thrown up his hands and sent it spinning far enough away that the road agents hadn't wanted to take time hunting for it.

And why should they? They had—again—stolen the mule Baransky had ridden and put close to a week's worth of food into their larder. It was a profitable and safe robbery. Who would notice if a few prospectors never reached the area with the most recent gold strike? Even if someone awaited them, they'd think news had come of a bigger, richer strike. And many would never make it across the pass, even in the better weather promised by springtime. The way to the other side of Desolation Mountain was treacherous at the best of times.

Leave a few dozen prospectors dead along the way, stealing their animals and equipment? It was easier than dynamiting fish in a barrel. The prospectors weren't likely to have it in mind to watch for ambushers until they reached the goldfields. Some might not even be armed.

Thinking about how easy it was for the road agents to work made Slocum even angrier. It was one thing robbing a stagecoach or holding up a bank. He had done those crimes himself when need demanded it or the temptation was simply too great to resist. But to intentionally murder men for a few paltry dollars gained by reselling their equipment at the base of the mountain gnawed at his gut like a tapeworm.

He got his feet under him and heaved. This time, other

than being a little shaky kneed, he stayed upright. Making his way to where his six-gun had fallen gave him time to recover his strength. He scooped up the pistol and held it in his hand. He tried to remember if the single shot he had fired had found a target. He couldn't. He wanted to have shot the son of a bitch but figured he would have to save that pleasure for another day.

Looking up at the sun caused a moment's uneasiness. When he figured out why, he became even angrier. He had lain in the meadow overnight. It was close to a full day after the ambush. That was the only explanation he had for the position of the sun. There had been only an hour or so of daylight remaining when he had found the meadow. Now there were three.

His belly growled from lack of food, and his mouth felt stuffed with cotton wool. Determining the passage of time from these clues proved elusive, but he had to think only one day had passed. If he had been out in the open for two days, creatures would have come and begun nipping away at his flesh.

Dusting off his hat, he walked back to where he had left the mule grazing peacefully. The hoofprints led toward the trail he had followed. Slocum considered trying to track on foot since it was a considerable distance back down the hill to the town. Instead, he found the faint traces of what he thought were Baransky's toes in the dirt and began following them again. He went back in the direction he had already taken, then pushed into thick undergrowth. Traces of cloth clung to thorn bushes, giving him an easy trail to follow. He detoured when he heard a brook gurgling across rocks some distance into the woods.

When he found the water, he drank his fill. The cold, clear runoff from higher on the mountain turned to ice in his belly. He didn't care. His backbone rubbed up against his stomach. Filling up even on water eased the hunger. Then he thrust his head into the stream and winced as the wound reopened. He laved off the dried blood and then kept his head underwater until the flesh tightened and the bleeding stopped. When he came up for air, he shook like a wet dog, sending droplets in all directions.

He felt better than he had since getting shot. And he was even more determined not to let the sons of bitches who had shot him and taken Clem Baransky get away with it.

The determination became more frustration when he got after their trail once more. In less than ten yards he found a small clearing where horses had been tethered. The outlaws had ridden away, probably with Baransky as their prisoner.

Slocum realized it wasn't going to avail him anything following the trail. He did anyway. Just as the sun dipped low and night turned chilly, he realized that he had taken a circuitous route back to the main track leading eventually up and over the mountain pass.

At the road, he looked in both directions, then decided. To return to Almost There a second time would be admitting failure. He had lost three men in his party. Although he couldn't say for certain, he believed Clem Baransky to be alive. Finding him would go a ways toward validating his sense of duty. Dead or alive didn't matter, but finding the would-be prospector did.

Barely had he gone a hundred yards when the lack of daylight began to work against him. Like it or not, he had to camp for the night. Shivering, he scooped out some dirt from around the roots of a piñon pine and worked his shoulders down so the wood protected him. The ground was cool but wouldn't get much colder. He wasn't likely to freeze, but it would be a long night.

Sleep came in short stretches, and when he did fall into deeper sleep, it was populated with nightmarish figures. Slocum thrashed about, once thinking he had been buried alive. It took a few seconds after his eyes popped open to realize he was still in the pine's wooden embrace. After that, he slept well enough to only feel cranky when he awoke around sunrise. He knew the time was late in the day since Desolation Mountain blocked the morning sun, but he wanted to know the exact time—and couldn't because the road agents had stolen his watch.

His brother Robert's watch. The only legacy he had of him.

Slocum pushed free of the roots and let the anger warm him. He got to his feet and started back on the trail, his belly grumbling at the lack of breakfast. There would be time later to forage. The mountainside was covered with growth at this altitude, and bitter early spring berries and other plants might be had if he wasn't too fussy about what he put into his mouth.

In spite of his determination, his legs weakened, forcing him to take a rest. As he perched on a rock looking ahead along up the trail, he saw a pair of travelers working their way upward. Using his hand to shield his eyes from the high sun, he still squinted. Then he found himself filled with mixed emotions. How two people could be so downright stupid was beyond him, but Stephen and Melissa Baransky had taken to the trail themselves and could be his salvation.

He dropped to the trail and began walking at a quicker clip in spite of his weariness. An hour later he overtook the brother and sister.

Slocum stopped and stared when he saw them sitting beside the road. Melissa comforted her brother, who appeared on the brink of tears. The brunette pushed a dirty strand of hair back and stared at him. For a moment, hope flared in those chocolate-colored eyes, then it died.

"You're on foot," she said.

"Where's your gear? Your mules?"

Stephen Baransky looked up. Anger replaced his tears. "You're responsible. You tried to rob us."

"And Mr. Gunnison did," Melissa said. The edge in her

voice told Slocum everything he needed to know. She might appear a hothouse flower, but given the chance, Melissa Baransky would skin a man alive and enjoy it. He didn't know who Gunnison was, but he'd hate to be the man if she caught him unawares.

"You were robbed, too," Slocum said. "I thought I saw your pa's trail. Turned out to be a trap, probably set by the men who kidnapped him."

"He's alive?" Melissa perked up.

"To hell with him. Gunnison stole *our* supplies. *Our* mules." Stephen rocked back and crossed his arms over his chest. With such a pose, he refused to allow any argument.

That was fine with Slocum. He didn't want to talk to Stephen.

He dropped beside Melissa.

"Tell me about this Gunnison."

"We decided to explore on our own," she said. "If you succeeded in finding Papa, well and good, but we would add to the chances of success. We hired him. He was recommended as a reputable guide."

"By the gent who sold me the mule?"

"Why, yes. You two were quite friendly. We thought it would be all right to do business with him and follow his suggestions."

"You thought that, Melly. I wanted to wait."

"It is just as well we didn't," she said primly, not bothering to even glance in her brother's direction. "Mr. Slocum has run aground, as have we."

"Nobody passed me going back down to the town," Slocum said, remembering what he could of the mountain terrain. "The men who dry-gulched me headed uphill."

"No one has passed us," she said.

"Then there's another trail that circles the mountain," he said. "There are plenty of meadows and game trails."

"You know where Gunnison went?"

"Why didn't he kill you?" Slocum looked at the woman. It wasn't hard since she was so beautiful, even with dirty hair and bedraggled clothing.

"It wasn't because he had a kindly streak, that's for certain sure," Stephen said. "He tried to kill me. Cut my throat! I swung at him until he finally ran off, like the craven he is!"

Slocum doubted the story, especially when Melissa caught her breath as if to correct her brother. More likely Gunnison had intended to take her for his own pleasure, and she had driven him off. Brother and sister might have fled into the darkness and Gunnison, maybe wounded, probably kicked in the balls at the least, had consoled himself with only taking their mules and gear.

"Bet Gunnison has a footprint about here"—Slocum grabbed his crotch—"and about the size of this shoe." He reached down and lifted Melissa's foot. She wasn't in a hurry to pull back out of his grip, but Stephen yanked her arm and caused her to lose her balance. She lay in the dirt, propped on her elbows, still studying Slocum.

"What are you going to do?" Stephen demanded. "I want justice!"

"Justice is kind of crude out here," Slocum said. "You willing to kill Gunnison?" He read the play of emotions on the young man's face well enough to know he lied when he answered.

"Yes!"

Slocum also read the intentions on his sister's face when she said in a low, choked voice, "Yes."

"I'll track him down since I have a good idea where he left the road. Might be the owlhoots who robbed me are headed to the same place."

"Same place? What do you mean?"

Slocum didn't answer Stephen. Instead he directed his question to his sister.

"You have any weapons?"

"None, Mr. Slocum."

He reached down and drew the thick-bladed knife he kept sheathed in his boot. Turning it around, he gave it to the woman handle first.

"Use it if you have to."

"Are you going to leave me your gun?" Stephen sounded put out that his sister had gotten something and he hadn't.

"I'll need it," was all Slocum answered.

He stood to go but found Melissa's hand gripping his arm.

"Are you sure you won't need this?" She held up the knife he had given her.

"Make a shelter and stay here. Don't go anywhere, especially back to town." He didn't want her running afoul of the merchant who dealt repeatedly in stolen mules and equipment. "I'll come back for you."

"How do we know that?" Stephen thrust out his chin, as if begging Slocum to take a swing at him.

"Because, Stephen dear, he said he would. Mr. Slocum is a man of his word. I can tell."

"Keep the knife," he told her, then turned and went down the trail without so much as a backward glance. If he had looked back at Melissa Baransky, his resolve might have faded. She had guaranteed that he would return by her words. He had made a promise to her, as he had a contract with her father. Both were binding.

Money might be forgotten and a business deal dissolved, but he had given his word to her. That was binding to the point he died.

Slocum slipped and slid down some of the steeper slopes in the road, but the height above lower stretches allowed him to see the faint tracks off the main trail. Several mules, maybe more, had followed that stretch.

He hoped this was the trail leading to a staging area where he could find not only Gunnison but the men who had robbed him and Clement Baransky, too. It took only a bit of skill to follow the spoor left behind. Gunnison made no effort to hide his passage, but why should he? Two greenhorns left alone on the mountain. How the brother and sister had survived the night, much less kept walking, was beyond Slocum, but he thought it probably had more to do with Melissa's determination than Stephen's courage.

A mile along the trail brought Slocum to a wooded area. Another mile into it he found a junction where several smaller trails joined a large one plunging directly ahead. From the crushed weeds and trampled dirt, quite a few men came this way regularly. Since it wasn't the trail over the mountain, it had to lead somewhere else that prospectors weren't inclined to explore.

Slocum was hesitant about continuing along the double-rutted road when it came to a long, narrow meadow. Anyone camped around the perimeter of the trees would spot him immediately. But this worked both ways. Slocum's hand flashed to his holstered six-gun when he saw a man with three mules resting in the shade not a quarter mile ahead and just off the road in the trees.

Slocum stepped back, found a game trail in the woods leading in the proper direction, and set off, stride long. As he walked, determination mounted. He had the chance to even the score and find out what was going on along the trail over Desolation Mountain.

Not that he didn't have a good idea. The gang working the trail robbed prospectors of their equipment, as they had the others in the party he had been hired to guide. If he had spent more time in town, he would have figured out that a guide's job also included being a bodyguard, but he had jumped at the chance to make easy money.

The thought of that money caused him to touch his empty vest pocket where the greenbacks had been stashed. His brother's watch, his poke, his supplies and mule—it had all been stolen. By now the mule was likely down in the merchant's corral, ready to be sold yet another time.

He slowed as he heard a stream running through the woods. Gunnison had camped not far from the water. This might have been luck on his part finding the spot in the road closest to the stream, but Slocum doubted it. More likely, Gunnison had robbed and pilfered before and had staked out this spot as his own to rest up.

Slocum heard the thief singing "Sweet Betsy from Pike" in a gravelly, off-key rendition. The discordant singing masked Slocum's footsteps as he approached through the woods, the stream at his back. Gunnison lay on his back, face to the sky, as he caterwauled.

Slocum was taken by surprise when the man looked down quickly, spotted him, and lifted a rifle hidden alongside his body.

"Been expecting you ever since I seen you on my trail." Gunnison lifted the rifle, Slocum square in his sights, and pulled the trigger.

6

The instant Gunnison stirred, Slocum dug his toes into the
dirt and launched himself. Even with his quick reflexes, he
almost died from the slug that ripped past him. He hit
the ground hard, rolled, and got off a quick shot at the treacherous guide. Gunnison, for all his bulk, moved as fast as
Slocum and came to a full sitting position.

Slocum kept rolling and firing. His aim was off, and
Gunnison wasn't the least bit scared of being hit. Slocum's
only luck came in the direction he had dived. He forced
Gunnison to twist about and fire awkwardly across his body,
never quite able to get a clean shot.

The last twist brought Slocum to his belly, elbows on the
ground for support. He squeezed off a round aimed straight
for the guide's face. The hammer fell on a dud. The metallic
click brought a snort of triumph from the guide.

Gunnison came to his knees, rifle butt snugged to his
shoulder.

"Don't know who you are, other 'n dead," Gunnison said.
He fired at the same time that Slocum cocked and fired
again.

Slocum winced as hot pain dragged along his left arm. He cocked his Colt for another shot but saw it wasn't necessary. His marksmanship proved superior to Gunnison's. The guide slumped, his rifle coming off his shoulder. Then he toppled to the side.

Getting to his feet gave Slocum passing agony from his wound, but he ignored it as he went to the body curled up in death. He kicked away the rifle, then prodded Gunnison with his boot. Slocum felt no triumph at surviving the gunfight. He had underestimated his opponent, and it had almost cost him his life. As he reloaded, he considered how stupid he had been since arriving at the base of Desolation Mountain.

Almost There might well be the way he had been thinking.

That was going to stop. He kicked Gunnison again just to be sure, then searched the man. He found almost a hundred dollars in greenbacks folded up and crammed into a coat pocket. These replenished his poke. He was still down a couple hundred dollars after being robbed, but again the tide was moving in his direction. He finished his search, almost hoping to find his brother's watch but knowing it wasn't likely.

Gunnison didn't have any watch on him but did carry a curious medallion. It had been a silver dollar but a bullet had drilled a hole through the center. Slocum held it up and peered through it, wondering at the reason the guide had carried it. The silver dollar got tucked away in his vest pocket, but Slocum continued to finger it through the cloth. Something about it and the man who had carried it didn't match. Shrugging it off, Slocum went about collecting the stolen gear and grabbed the reins of the mules.

It took a few minutes for him to settle the nervous animals. Too much shooting had spooked them. He swung onto the back of the sturdiest of the trio and started back toward the main road, where he had left Melissa and her brother, only to stop and think. He frowned as too many unanswered questions bedeviled him. His curiosity had gotten him into trouble before, but now he had more than his promise to Melissa to keep. Her pa's body had never been found. While it might be in a ravine where he could never find it, Slocum had the gut feeling from all he had seen in the meadow before he was ambushed that Clem Baransky was still alive.

Why? What made him worth saving when the road agents were inclined to shoot down any prospector they came across to steal their equipment? And Gunnison had followed a trail known to him that turned into a road as well traveled as the one up to Desolation Pass.

Turning around, Slocum looked over his shoulder in the direction Gunnison had been traveling. A gut feeling about the road and the murderous guide told him that something lay around the mountain, just out of sight. If Baransky hadn't been killed outright, had he been taken as a prisoner along this road? Slocum closed his eyes and imagined the scene. Baransky, hands tied as he rode surrounded by three road agents, vanishing into the woods at the far end of the clearing.

Where did the road lead?

Slocum winched as he turned back to face the path that would return him to the main road. His wound throbbed constantly and sent a stab of pain all the way down his left arm as he moved. Getting into another fight would be risky.

What lay beyond the woods? Would he find Clem Baransky there?

For a moment, he considered his duty to Melissa and her brother. He had recovered their stolen mules and equipment, but he owed their pa more. If Clem Baransky had been taken prisoner, did the owlhoots holding guns on the man expect a ransom? That hardly seemed likely from the way Stephen had been reluctant to spend even a dime more than necessary. Melissa seemed to be the family member intent on finding their father while Stephen was only along for the ride.

Slocum reversed his course and rode in the direction Gunnison had taken. Before he left the meadow, he tethered two mules with their supplies out of sight in the woods. Only then did he press on, riding the surefooted mule that had been Gunnison's. The road curled through the woods, then bent around the rocky bulk of the mountain. For more than two hours he rode, every foot along the road taking him into new countryside. This area proved less steep than the western slope of the mountain and the road was even more worn with hooves. More than one trail came up from lower elevations, making it seem as if this was the crossroads.

Even as he discovered more, Slocum worried about whether he had done the right thing leaving Melissa and Stephen the way he had. He ought to have ridden back with their mules, then sent them . . . where?

If they returned to town, they were sitting ducks. More men than the merchant were involved in the thefts. Seeing supposed victims return would send shock waves throughout the outlaw organization. Certainly questions would be asked of the two—questions for which they had no good answers.

All it would take would be for one of them, probably Stephen if Slocum read the man right, to mention that Slocum was still on the mountainside hunting for Clem Baransky. That would be like pouring boiling water down an anthill. Every outlaw working as a scavenger along the trail would be out for Slocum's scalp.

Better to let brother and sister stew a bit, because Slocum felt he was getting close to an answer about their pa's fate. Blocking the road ahead rose a palisade. The gate was ajar, but Slocum saw men moving on the other side. Too late to retreat and make a stealthier approach, he rode on boldly. If he couldn't talk his way past, he could start slinging lead. He was in enough pain from his wounds not to care who got killed.

"Whoa, mister, you stop that there mule of yours," a man said, coming through the gate. He walked easy and carried a rifle in the crook of his left arm. There didn't seem to be any hint he recognized Slocum or had orders to shoot on sight.

Slocum did as he was told, aware of several rifle barrels poking through loopholes in the palisade. He'd better do some fancy talking because shooting would only win him an early grave.

"Where you headin', mister?"

"Through there. To the other side of your fence."

The man laughed so hard that the tips of his well-waxed handlebar mustache unfurled, leaving fuzzy ends.

"Of course you want to get on through. They all do. You got the toll?"

"How much?"

For some reason, that caused the guard to swing his rifle around and aim it in Slocum's general direction.

"Mister, if this is where you want to ride, you know the answer to that."

Slocum considered the greenbacks in his pocket. That might be enough to bribe his way past. He doubted simply riding back the way he came was safe. Any of the riflemen could put a bullet in his spine—and likely would.

"Got this," Slocum said, pulling out the silver dollar with the hole shot through it. He flipped it so it spun about in the air and reached for his six-shooter at the same time.

The guard deftly caught the coin, barely looked at it before tossing it back.

"Why didn't you say so? No need to get us all het up." The guard stepped out of his way, and the rifles disappeared from the loopholes.

Slocum wasn't sure what had happened, but the plugged silver dollar was a ticket past the guards. He tucked the coin safely into his pocket and rode through, looking neither left nor right. He rounded a bend in the road a hundred yards from the fence before he let out his breath in an explosive gasp. Lady luck finally rode on his shoulder. He had thought the silver dollar might be melted down to a nugget and swapped for real coins—smaller ones. Never had he considered it to be the key that opened a gateway to . . .

. . . an entire city.

He halted the mule and stared. Nestled in a saddle of a pass that led back deeper into the hills lay a town equal in size to the one at the base on the other side of Desolation Mountain. There didn't seem to be as much commercial activity but the buildings were numerous, and he saw several large saloons along the main street. Side streets meandered off to one-story houses. From the horses and mules tethered, there might be a population of several hundred living here.

Before he urged his mule on, he cocked his head to one side. A faint sound teased him, then disappeared. He couldn't put a name to it, but it was familiar. Slocum waited another few seconds, but it never sounded again.

He rode down the center of the broad street, taking in every detail. Like the other town, this one had no name he could discern, but it was as much a boomtown with the buildings thrown up higgledy-piggledy. Most buildings canted to one side or the other and the saloon to his right might have been built by a drunk carpenter. Nowhere did he see a perfect square. The doorway appeared to have been stepped on by a giant and squeezed to one side but was wide enough for three men to enter side by side. Nails had been used liberally to hold it all together, though some cracks between planks were large enough for Slocum to slide his hand through.

One strong wind would topple many of the buildings, but from the men coming and going. he saw no real concern. Most were dressed as cowboys and all wore their iron high up on their hip. A few carried their six-shooters lower, tied down onto their thigh like a gunfighter. From the cold stares he got from them, he doubted many had ridden herd or plowed a field.

As he rode, Slocum was aware of men glancing at him,

but that was the full extent of their scrutiny. They paid him no attention other than he was riding down the street. Strangers weren't to be feared—he guessed most everyone in this town rated that appellation.

This was the kind of place where kidnappers brought men to hold for ransom. But how was he going to find Baransky and the men who had grabbed him out on the trail?

"You got more 'n that mangy mule yer ridin'?" The call came from a gent rocked back in a chair, precariously leaning against the saloon wall. "You got more, I kin make you a good deal."

Slocum tugged on the reins and walked his mule to where he could study the man.

"Might have a few mules and some gear. Who else is buying?"

"Why, mister, you don't need nobody else. Ole Buddy Drew—that's me—gives top dollar."

That told Slocum more of what he needed to know. The town thrived on buying stolen animals and supplies. That it competed and obviously thrived along with Almost There told of the huge numbers of men and supplies struggling to the distant goldfields. He hesitated, a faint sound alerting him.

"What's wrong, mister? You got a bug in yer ear?"

"Hear something."

"All you need to hear's my offer cuz it'll be the best you can git in this godforsaken town. You got them other mules to show me? I don't buy no pig in a poke."

"Buy me a drink and let's dicker," Slocum said. He dismounted, wondering how safe the mule would be if he left it in the street. Barely had his feet touched the muddy ground when a grizzled man in a threadbare old Confederate uniform limped up. His left leg was nigh on useless from the way he dragged himself along.

"Watch it fer a dime," he said.

"Git yer lazy ass outta here, Wallace. You don't want to annoy this fellow. He's got stuff to sell."

"Here," Slocum said. "Don't let anybody make off with the mule or saddle." He handed the gimpy man a greenback. The sneer told him scrip wasn't held in high esteem in these parts.

"This'll buy you a half hour, no more."

Slocum nodded. His business wouldn't take him that long. He'd either find out what Buddy Drew knew or be on his way quick enough.

"You come right on in, mister. What do I call you?" Drew held the saloon door open for Slocum.

"Thirsty."

Drew laughed, but there was no humor in it. He called out to the barkeep, "Set 'em up, Mr. Preston. Me and my friend here got business to discuss."

The bartender wiped off a pair of shot glasses using a rag, which disappeared back behind the bar. Slocum doubted it was much cleaner than the glasses that were quickly filled to the brim with amber fluid.

"Bottoms up," Drew said, knocking back his shot.

Slocum was slower to follow. A drop of chloral hydrate would leave him unconscious on the floor and at the mercy of the men scattered around the saloon watching him like a hungry coyote watches a plump rabbit. He snorted as the fiery liquor slid down his gullet.

"Potent stuff, ain't it?"

Slocum waited a moment for any hint of dizziness. Drew would be the first to die if he had been drugged. But the burning in his belly didn't warn him of anything wrong, other than his lack of food recently.

"I'll swap the mules I got," Slocum said.

"Swap? I don't understand. I run a strictly cash business. Ask any of the boys." Drew made a sweeping gesture that took in everyone.

"I want information. I got a score to settle with an owl-hoot and heard he was here."

"What kind of score?" Drew looked at him as he stepped back a half pace.

"That's between me and Baransky."

"That his name? Baransky?"

"Clem Baransky."

"Don't know him. Any of you know this Baransky fellow?"

Drew never took his eyes off Slocum but still answered, "Sorry, they don't know him. You got to look elsewhere, though I'm still willin' to buy yer stock."

"Two mules. What price?"

"Got to see 'em first. You came into town alone."

"I'll look around a bit more," Slocum said.

"You're not walkin' 'way from this deal."

"What deal?"

"You drank my whiskey. That sealed the deal. You lyin' 'bout havin' more mules? That means you're tryin' to cheat me."

Drew stepped back and pulled his coat away from the six-shooter slung at his hip.

"You willing to die over this?" Slocum asked.

He saw that Buddy Drew was from the way he flexed his fingers.

Slocum squared off, a cold calm settling over him.

7

"Why don't you jist give ole Buddy Drew that mule and we kin call it even-steven?" The man's fingers twitched again, and Slocum knew no deal was going to happen that didn't also include swapping a few ounces of lead.

"I'll pay for the drink."

"Sure you—" Drew's hand stopped twitching as he went for his iron. Talking while drawing might have stayed some men's hand but not John Slocum's.

His fingers closed around the ebony butt of his Colt as he turned slightly to his right. The six-gun slid from his cross-draw holster and fired almost in the same blink of an eye. The white smoke filled the room, then had even more added as Drew fired.

But Slocum saw his slug had been enough, and there was no need for a second shot. A small red splotch spread on Drew's chest. He reached out to support himself on the bar with his left hand, but his right was too weak to hold his six-shooter. It clattered to the floor, resting inches from where his bullet had torn a path through the boards. He followed his weapon to the floor and lay unmoving.

Looking around, Slocum hunted for anyone who would take advantage of the situation and gun him down. The few men in the saloon who had been disturbed by the gunfight turned away. Only two were interested enough to wander over, more curious than angry that one of their own had been killed.

A man dressed in miner's garb looked down, scratched himself, then asked, his eyes never leaving Drew's body, "You mind if we help him on out of here?"

Slocum shook his head. He kept the six-shooter in his grip, waiting to see what happened. A harsh laugh escaped his lips when he saw the two men dive down on the fallen crook and begin rummaging through his pockets. When a bright gold watch appeared, Slocum stepped out and grabbed it.

He held it up, then let it spin slowly on its chain.

He dropped it into the scavenger's outstretched hand and said, "Thought it was mine."

"Mine now," the scavenger said gleefully, tucking it away. He and his partner made rapid work of stripping anything of value from the carcass.

"Git him on outta here," the barkeep said, showing his first interest since pouring the drinks. "It's bad for business to leave bodies around like that."

"He's all yers, mister," one scavenger said, looking up at Slocum.

"Do what you want with him. You've been paid." Slocum pointed with his six-gun. The movement caused one to slip and sit down hard. The other fumbled for his own six-shooter, then thought better of it.

"You heard him. Buddy's all yers. Take him on out the back way. Now, dammit, do it now!" The barkeep slammed his fist down hard on the bar, causing the empty shot glasses to jump. He looked over at Slocum and asked, "Want another?"

Slocum slid his six-shooter back into the holster and left

without saying another word. Chances were good the drink would have cost him more than the price of the whiskey. This one would have been laced with a Mickey Finn.

It was that kind of drinking emporium.

He stepped out, shooing Wallace out of his way. The man had been peering around the corner of the doorway watching everything that happened inside.

"You kilt him. You got a quick hand, mister. Kin I work fer you?"

Slocum started to laugh, then considered how difficult it would be finding anything in this town. The palisade and armed guards told him this was closer to a prison than a town.

"Get yourself a bottle and come back out and join me." He handed Wallace a couple of the greenbacks and examined the chairs along the boardwalk. He found one that would support his weight without collapsing. He had barely sat in it when Wallace returned. A couple inches were already missing from the bottle.

Wallace saw his interest in the bottle and hastily said, "Damned bartender's always cheatin' me. Says this is what passes for a full bottle." He held it out to Slocum, who took it, pulled the cork, and tipped the bottle up enough to wet his lips. They stung like fire. He handed the bottle back.

"Help yourself," Slocum invited. "Now that Drew's out of business, who should I see about selling spare mules and gear?"

"Oh, that's easy 'nuff," Wallace said, sinking into the rickety chair beside Slocum. He took a quick drink, then another, and passed the bottle back. Slocum held up his hand, showing he wasn't interested in the tarantula juice.

This suited Wallace just fine. The liquor lubricated his tongue.

"Trueheart runs the whole damn place. Not sure what he's up to, but it's changin' as we sit here jawin'."

"Changing?"

"Used to be the fellows went out and found equipment dropped along the trail over the pass."

"Dropped?"

"Early on, prospectors didn't have good sense and loaded theyselves down with ever' contrivance you could imagine. Pickin' up after 'em was profitable. Hell, I done some of it myself."

Slocum barely paid attention as the story unfolded. From scavenging, the men had turned into road agents and outright killers. Who was to know or care? But the flow of stolen goods had become too great to use so they had taken up selling it over and over in Almost There at the base of the mountain.

"Trueheart think that up?"

"Not much he don't think on, mister. He's a deep one. Another nip?"

Slocum took another swig to keep Wallace happy and give him the feeling he had a drinking companion. Given the chance, Wallace would be as happy draining the entire bottle on his own.

"What happens when the goldfields over Desolation Pass peter out?"

Wallace looked at him with one eye closed, the better to focus. He lifted a grimy finger to his lips and whispered, "Shush."

"You said more was going on. What's Trueheart up to?"

"Somethin' real big. Dunno what, but them folks all around him are abuzz with it. Been kinda strange, too, lately. A lot of supplies comin' into town what could be sold never get traded. Don't know what Trueheart is doin' with 'em but he's got enough food and equipment carried off to supply an army. Think they been buildin' something, but nobody knows what. Nobody not in tight with Trueheart."

"How's that?" Slocum pushed the bottle back when Wallace tried to give it to him again. The man didn't think

Slocum was unneighborly at all. Probably the contrary from the hefty drink he took, then belched.

"Lot of equipment taken out on the trail's not goin' downhill no more. Even keepin' mules 'stead of sellin' 'em below."

Slocum saw he wasn't getting any more information out of an increasingly besotted Wallace.

"You did good looking after my mule," Slocum said, standing. "Keep the rest of the bottle."

"You're a prince 'mong men, mister. Anythin' more I kin do, you look up ole Wallace and I'll be there to help."

Slocum mounted his mule and rode away from the saloon, going deeper into the heart of the town. For a moment he thought he heard a strange noise again but his braying mule drowned out any chance he had of identifying it.

He took the first cross street and saw a huge building that had to be Trueheart's headquarters. From the armed men standing guard outside, he knew better than to barge in on the man responsible for building the whole damned town. He rode past, took a smaller street into the red light district, then made his way to a switchback trail leading upward into the low hills just above town. From a level spot along the trail, he got a good view of the claptrap buildings—and Trueheart's headquarters.

He stepped down from the mule and sat on a rock, letting the animal graze while he watched the ebb and flow of men and supplies throughout the town. It seemed to him that more went to Trueheart's building than was needed and what came out were pack mules laden with canvas-masked loads.

Since Trueheart provided a clearinghouse for everything stolen along the trail over the mountain, all Slocum got from this was that another trail down to the town below existed. Trueheart didn't want to spook the prospectors working their way up the steep hill by blatantly showing the stolen equipment being returned. Some of the parties had to be heavily armed and not worth the effort to steal from.

Unlike the party of four Slocum had been hired to guide across Desolation Pass.

That rankled as bad as an infected tooth. He should have known there would be outlaws along the trail and yet he had ignored the risk and it had cost three men their lives. And what had happened to Clement Baransky? Slocum thought he had been brought to Trueheart's town. But why? And how could he find him?

The sun began sinking fast since this town was situated around the mountainside away from the trail used by the prospectors. Dawn came earlier here, but twilight cloaked the town sooner in retaliation.

He decided he had to get a look into Trueheart's headquarters, no matter what the risk.

He took his time returning to the town. Unlike many towns, no gaslights blazed to illuminate the streets. Using the shadows to his benefit, he worked his way closer to the large, well-lit building that was four or five times the size of a big barn. And behind it was a regular-sized barn where the men stabled their animals.

Slocum left his mule tethered in a spot he hoped wouldn't be noticed by an itinerant thief, then went directly to the barn. Several men finished currying their horses and headed in a loose group to Trueheart's main building. Slocum trailed them, trying not to look conspicuous. The men were tired from the trail and didn't josh with one another. They came to the back door of the huge building, and here Slocum hesitated.

Two guards just inside scrutinized everyone entering.

He found himself caught in a trap. If he turned and walked off, he would draw attention. But if he tried to bull his way inside, bullets might fly. Seeing the situation, he made a quick decision and boldly walked in behind a short, bowlegged cowboy.

"Wait," a guard said. "Don't know you."

Slocum reached into his vest pocket and pulled out the

silver dollar with a hole shot through it. This had been his ducat to get past the palisades.

"Go on," the guard said, eying the mutilated coin and paying Slocum no heed.

Slocum followed the last of the men down a narrow corridor and into a large barracks. As he got a better look, he thought he had entered an army post quartermaster's storage room. Lining the walls, shelves held about every piece of mining and prospecting equipment he had ever seen. Chisels, picks, hammers, all there. He frowned when he saw carbide lamps, rope, miners' candles, even cases of blasting powder. More than prospecting equipment was stashed here. Trueheart kept mining equipment fit for cutting shafts and blowing down rock walls to follow a subterranean, meandering vein of gold.

"What you need, mister?"

"I was thinking of some dynamite," Slocum said, looking back over his shoulder at a mousy man wearing a green eyeshade and a shirt that had been white once. He had worn it until it turned gray, and in spite of wearing cuff protectors, the cuffs were frayed. Black stains on the man's short fingers revealed his true occupation. He was an accountant.

"Nope, not for sale."

"Trade? I got a couple mules."

"We got all the animals for the project we need."

Slocum wanted to ask what this "project" was but knew better than to betray ignorance.

"What you need for the project? I can furnish it special."

"We got a dozen men out on the trail doing just that."

"Let me look over the goods," Slocum said. "You got a customer to tend." He pointed to a man dressed in canvas pants and a denim shirt running his fingers over a carbide light.

The accountant mumbled to himself and went to dicker with the miner for the lamp. Slocum saw a small leather bag change hands. The accountant and the miner crossed the large room to a table where a small balance scale determined the value of the bag's contents.

"Gold dust," Slocum said softly.

He went to the shelves and took down a chisel and hammer to avoid drawing unwanted attention. A murmur passed through the men in the room, causing Slocum to look around.

A tall, whipcord-thin man dressed in a fancy cutaway coat, green brocade vest with dangling gold chains, top hat making him close to seven feet tall, and boots shined so hard they reflected like mirrors strutted into the room. Four men flanked him. From their look, they were bodyguards and positioned themselves in such a way that their boss wasn't accosted by men moving in his direction like iron filings to a magnet.

Slocum didn't need a formal introduction to know who this was.

"You gents finding what you need? If you don't, ask Mr. Peltier over there." Trueheart pointed at the accountant, who smiled wanly at the introduction.

Trueheart made his way through the room, talking with some men and clapping others on the shoulder before moving on as a monarch might after greeting his vassals. Slocum turned back to the array of equipment to keep from attracting Trueheart's notice. Wallace had said something different was passing through this town. Slocum stood in a room that gave testimony to that. He doubted Wallace or most of the citizens ever came here, yet this had to reflect a huge number of thefts—and deaths—along the trail up to Desolation Pass.

Trueheart had gone from being a carrion eater to a hunter. Exactly what he used all this equipment for meant he had moved on past even this. To what?

"What time's it getting to be, Hersh?"

Slocum fought to keep his instinctive reaction from getting

him killed. Trueheart's bodyguard pulled out a watch, flipped open the case, and studied the face before telling his boss.

That watch was Slocum's.

Trueheart glanced in Slocum's direction, drawn by his jerky action. Slocum lowered his eyes and clutched the hammer and chisel he had taken off the shelf, as if he were more interested in them than Trueheart or his henchman.

"You. You're new here, aren't you?"

Slocum looked up and locked eyes with Trueheart.

"Just got in."

"Do tell. You're not working the project?"

"Want to," Slocum said.

"Got all we need there," Trueheart said. "You keep on bringing in what we need and might be one day you can work there."

Hersh nudged his boss and whispered for a few seconds. Trueheart looked exasperated, as if silently acknowledging a king's duty never ended. Without another word to Slocum, he went to the table where Peltier weighed out his gold dust and got into a heated discussion with the accountant.

Slocum put back the hammer and chisel and headed for the doorway leading back outside. If he stayed any longer, he would get himself in big trouble. He had a good look at Hersh and knew he had to be the one who had robbed him out in the meadow. His steps slowed when he remembered why he had come into the building.

Clem Baransky.

Hersh had to know what happened to the man he had grabbed out on the trail. Slocum watched as Trueheart's henchman stood a pace away from the table and Peltier. Would Hersh recognize him as the pilgrim he had left for dead?

How he could cut Hersh out of the herd was a poser. But he had to try if he wanted to find Baransky.

Slocum stepped out into the cold night air and looked around. A slow smile crossed his lips when he saw the perfect place to ambush Hersh.

8

Two horses were saddled and waiting behind a fancy carriage near the barn. Slocum wanted to examine the vehicle more closely. In the darkness, its gold designs seemed to have been painted on. Considering how flamboyantly Trueheart dressed, however, his carriage might have had actual gold leaf glued on it—and Slocum had no doubt that Trueheart was its owner. It fit the man too perfectly to belong to anyone else.

Slocum pressed himself against the side of the barn, melting into shadows, when Trueheart and his henchmen came from the large building. Hersh spoke in tones too low for Slocum to overhear, but what he said displeased Trueheart.

"Don't bother me with that. You take care of it."

"Drew was a good supplier," Hersh said. Slocum caught his breath. He had gunned down one of Trueheart's men, but considering the way this town was run, that wasn't unlikely. Everyone in it was in Trueheart's gang in some way or another.

"Get whoever cut him down and enlist him," Trueheart said, getting into the carriage. It creaked under his weight.

It creaked even more when one bodyguard got into the back and sat cross-legged. Another grabbed the reins, snapped them loudly, and drove off, leaving Hersh and the fourth guard behind.

"What you intend to do, Hersh?"

"Damned if I know. From what the barkeep said, the owlhoot who gunned down Buddy was a tough customer."

"Might be Trueheart is right. Hire him."

"I liked Buddy."

"You was skimmin' half of what he made 'fore it ever got to Trueheart."

"You shut that pie hole. Don't ever say that out loud. Trueheart might not know you're kidding."

"Who's kidding? I know you and Drew had an arrangement. I want in. Let me be the buyer and we kin split fifty-fifty."

Slocum edged closer as Hersh and the bodyguard argued.

"You're a damned thief, Mackley."

"But I'm an honest thief. I stay bought."

They argued a bit more, then Hersh said, "Get on out of here. Trueheart will wonder what became of you."

"I'll see to the buyin' come daybreak. Thanks, partner." Mackley laughed as he rode after the carriage.

Hersh worked to cinch down the belly strap on his horse, then half turned when Slocum came up behind him.

"What do you—"

Hersh grunted as Slocum slammed the barrel of his Colt into the side of his head. He sagged, dropped to one knee, and rubbed his temple. Slocum slugged him again, driving him to the ground. His horse crow hopped and tried to bolt, but Hersh somehow clung to the dangling reins.

"We need to talk." Slocum reached over and plucked his watch from Hersh's pocket.

"Who the hell are you?" Hersh rubbed the side of his head and tried to focus. "You're gonna pay for this. You know who I am?"

"You're the man who kidnapped Clem Baransky."

"What? Who's that?"

Slocum hesitated. Hersh was still disoriented from the buffaloing and wasn't likely to lie easily or quickly.

"A prospector you grabbed out on the trail over the mountain," he explained. "Is he in town?"

"I don't know who you mean."

Slocum hit him again, knocking him flat on his back. He stood over him with his Colt Navy cocked and aimed between his eyes.

"The men you kidnap out on the trail. What happens to them?"

"Th-They're not in town. I swear it!"

Slocum frowned. There was a ring of truth in Hersh's words, but—

Hersh hooked one toe around the back of Slocum's right foot and kicked like a mule, catching him on the kneecap. Slocum lost his balance, but as he fell, he jerked off a shot. He sat hard on the ground and worked to cock his pistol for another shot. There was no need for that. Hersh wasn't moving. Slocum rubbed his bruised knee and swung around. His bullet had snuffed out Hersh's life in a split second, going straight through his forehead.

He got to his feet and dusted himself off. Then he heard hoofbeats coming back fast from the direction Mackley had ridden.

"What's going on, Hersh? You all right?"

Slocum considered taking Hersh's horse since it would give him a faster escape, then realized it would also brand him as both a killer and a horse thief. Even in a law-abiding town, he wasn't likely to escape a noose with any story when the evidence was against him. He faded into the shadows again, six-gun in his hand and hanging at his side.

Mackley jumped from the saddle and went to his slain partner. He drew his six-shooter and looked around, but he didn't make any move toward Slocum. When he knelt and began going through Hersh's pockets, taking what money was there, Slocum knew there was no honor among these thieves. Hersh's death only meant that Mackley moved up in the hierarchy of scavengers.

Mackley snared the dangling reins and led the horse over to his own. With a quick vault, he was again in the saddle and rode off, Hersh's horse trotting along behind.

Slocum moved cautiously, wary of anyone else who might have heard the gunshot. Business went on as usual in the large building, and nobody was in the barn. He returned to his mule, stepped up, and began the slow walk toward the gate leading back to the main trail.

He had tried to find Clem Baransky and had failed. But he patted his vest pocket where his watch rode safely once more and smiled. The excursion hadn't been a complete waste of time. He had killed one man who might have been responsible for dry-gulching him on the trail and had put a bullet through the head of another who not only had been part of the ambush but had also robbed him.

He was pleased with that. But where was Clem Baransky?

With a snap of the reins, he kept his mule moving. Wherever he was, it wasn't in this town.

Slocum pushed back his hat and stared in surprise. Stephen and Melissa Baransky had done as he'd asked and stayed put. He kicked at the flanks of his tired mule and tugged on the reins of the other two he had retrieved.

"Mr. Slocum! You're back!" Melissa turned to her brother and said, "See? I told you he wouldn't abandon us!"

Stephen grumbled some but came over and took the reins from Slocum.

"Didn't think you were coming back."

"I gathered as much," Slocum said, slipping his leg over the mule's back and dropping to the rocky ground. He ached all over. The mule's gait was different from a horse's. He could ride all day, half into the night, and do it again when the sun rose, but not on a mule. They were surefooted and ornery cusses intent on inflicting as much agony on a rider as possible.

"What happened? Did you have to . . . fight? To get the supplies back?" Melissa's brown eyes glowed with excitement. He wondered what would happen to that sparkle if he told her he had killed not only Gunnison but two other road agents.

"I got everything back," he said, "but I didn't find your pa. No trace of him."

That still rankled.

"Then he might be on the trail, ahead of us. A long ways ahead of us," Melissa said with some sadness. She turned and stared up the trail where it disappeared around a bend. They had reached a point where the initial steep slope petered out, giving a chance for a few miles of easy climbing, but from what Slocum had seen of a map, after that the going got hard. Fast.

"What's so all-fired important that you have to reach your pa?"

"He wants to talk us out of going on, Melly."

"I want you to think about how hard it'll be just reaching Desolation Pass. From there into the goldfields isn't an easy jaunt either."

"We have to give Papa the sad news." Melissa took a deep sigh. The movement of her bodice distracted Slocum so much he almost missed her tiny voice saying, "Mama is dead. And only he can square things with the estate."

"Estate?"

"There's no reason to explain family finances to the likes of *him*," Stephen said, almost spitting out the words.

"Please," she said, ignoring her brother's outburst. "Mr. Slocum has to know whether to continue with us or return to town."

For a moment Slocum's head spun. Return to town? Then

he realized she meant Almost There at the base of the mountain. She knew nothing of the one run by Trueheart and his gang.

Leaving that town built on thievery still bothered him. He touched the lump made by his watch to reassure himself it still rode safely in his vest pocket. But whatever Trueheart did was a mystery he wished he could have solved. Although Hersh ended up dying, he had blurted out that there weren't any kidnapped prospectors in the town—and Slocum believed that. Hersh had been taken by surprise by the question and his answer had a ring of honesty to it. That might well have been the only time Trueheart's henchman had not lied or connived.

That left Slocum to wonder about Clement Baransky. The place where the ambush had occurred was obvious. Finding Baransky's mule once more at the bottom of the trail gave mute testimony to something bad happening to him. But there hadn't been a body, and evidence of someone having been dragged off was real. Why should the scavengers fake that when they believed no one would notice or care?

Slocum looked past the woman up the trail. As incredible as it seemed, Clem Baransky might have escaped and continued on the trail.

"He might have fallen off the mule," Stephen said, breaking Slocum's thoughts.

"I suppose so. If he fell off, the mule could have been found by someone else and taken back down the hill." Slocum didn't believe that for a moment since it didn't explain the drag marks he had seen in the meadow where Baransky's mule must have been stolen, but the way Melissa's face lit with hope kept him talking. It was cruel to give her a dream of finding her pa alive, but he felt undercurrents running between brother and sister that bothered him.

Stephen wanted to hear that his pa was dead. He never said it, but the way he spoke convinced Slocum of that.

"Who gets the inheritance if your pa's not found?"

"Melly, be quiet!"

She turned on her brother and glared at him, moving close enough so they were inches apart.

"No, Stephen, *you* hush up. You've dragged your feet the entire way. I refuse to believe Papa is dead. Oh, sure, his mule was back in the corral, but we haven't found a body. You know how strong Papa can be. He never gives up."

"You saw the two expeditions that passed us, Melly. You saw them. There wasn't a one in either party that wouldn't have chewed up Pa and eaten him for breakfast. They are hard men. He didn't know what he was getting into."

"He knew because he has dealt with men like that all his life," she said, stamping her foot. "He's not dead. I won't let him be."

"If your brother's saying you ought to go on back down the trail, he's right. I can keep searching. You have your mules and supplies."

"That's mighty dangerous, Mr. Slocum. Stephen's right about the men we saw being such hard cases. They might rob us as we passed them going down."

He said nothing to that. The other prospectors were likely the least of the problems brother and sister would face returning to Almost There. Trueheart's men still plied their thieving trade along this stretch of the trail. Men would be tuckered out after the first steep slope and present easy pickings. Anyone going down would draw attention—and guns.

"I'll escort you back. This isn't any place for two greenhorns."

Melissa spun on him, her face turning up to glare at him as she had with her brother. To emphasize her point, she balled her fists and put them on her hips to give the very picture of determination.

"I am my father's daughter. He would never give up on a dream. I will never give up hope until I find him. Alive, I pray, but if he is dead, I intend to give him a Christian burial. But one way or the other, *I will find him!*"

"You'd go on without a guide?"

"Some guide you are," grumbled Stephen.

"I will. We will," she said.

"I'll see you to the goldfields on the other side of the pass, but if nobody's seen your pa, you'll give up and go back home. That's my deal."

"Very well," she said somewhat contritely.

"And you won't spend more 'n a week hunting for him," Slocum said. From the way Melissa spoke, she would insist on interrogating every prospector within twenty miles. That way lay madness and disappointment.

"That hardly seems long enough."

"It'll seem like forever by the time we reach the pass," Slocum said.

"Then we have a bargain." Melissa thrust out her tiny hand. Slocum's engulfed hers, but she had a firm handshake to seal their pact.

Slocum wondered if he would have agreed to such a wild-goose chase if he hadn't felt guilty about losing not only her pa but the other three in the party. He didn't know, and that bothered him.

"Now that you've fetched our mules, we can push on right away," she said.

"Getting dark in less than an hour. Let's get some food, rest up, and then hit the trail the first thing in the morning."

"Morning comes so late on this side of the mountain," she said.

"All the more reason to rest up so we can make better time."

Stephen sputtered about something obscene, but Slocum ignored him. So did Melissa. Over Melissa's objections, he fixed dinner from the supplies he had recovered from Gunnison, then cleaned up the tin plates in the nearby stream.

"I'll put my bedroll over there," Melissa said, studying the terrain carefully. "You can sleep near the mules, Stephen. We don't want them stolen in the night."

"Let Slocum sleep with the animals. He's used to it."

Before Slocum could respond, Melissa cut him off.

"He will be up on that prominence so he can watch the trail in both directions. Someone needs to remain alert and stand watch so we aren't killed in our sleep."

"By prospectors?" scoffed Stephen.

"Or by highwaymen or Indians. I heard there are Indians roaming about these mountains. Isn't that right, Mr. Slocum?"

Something in the way she spoke made him agree. It had been a year or more since the Blackfoot had kicked up a ruckus. The Nez Perce were farther west the last he had heard and no threat. But she certainly spoke the truth about other prospectors stealing from them, and he had no doubt Mackley and others from Trueheart's town would prowl the trail looking for easy pickings.

"All right," Stephen said with ill grace.

Like a mother hen, Melissa bustled about, getting everyone to the proper spot, then spread her bedroll and lay down, pointedly drawing the blanket over her shoulders.

Slocum, atop the small rise, laced his fingers under his head and watched the stars pop out, sharp and hard and brilliant. A gentle breeze began blowing and thin, high clouds crossed the stars, turning the sky to gauze studded with rhinestones. As he was drifting off to sleep, he heard a faint movement from the direction of the camp. He reached over and drew his six-shooter, then rolled onto his back and waited.

He saw a dim figure moving toward him up the gentle slope. A deep whiff of the night breeze caused him to lower the hammer on his Colt and slip it back into the holster beside his head so she would never know.

But she did.

His blanket fluttered up and then was pulled back down as Melissa snuggled close to him.

"You were going to shoot me," she accused.

"Not after I caught a whiff of your perfume."

"I'm not wearing any."

He rolled over and took her in his arms. She fit nicely, softness against his hard body crushing in all the right spots. Inhaling deeply, he caught the scent of a woman.

"You don't need perfume. You smell just fine this way."

"I want to thank you for going along, John," she said softly, her face buried in his chest.

But it was not her face or lips working to kiss against his flesh that aroused him. Her nimble fingers worked on the buttons holding his fly closed. He gasped when she succeeded in finding what lay behind the thick denim.

"You're hard already," she said.

"You do that to me. Never seen a woman so pretty."

"Liar. I bet you've seen plenty of women prettier than me. All of them. Without a stitch of clothing on." She began squeezing rhythmically, encouraging him to become even harder in the circle of her fingers. When he was steely enough for her, she began stroking up and down slowly.

"This is what I want, John. Only not between my fingers. In me. I want to feel you moving inside me. With this."

He gulped as she squeezed down hard around his manhood.

"Keep doing that and I might not last long enough."

She giggled and said, "Why do I doubt that? You're not a young buck. You've had women. Plenty of them, unless I miss my guess."

"And you still want me to do this to you?"

He reached down and lifted her skirt. His hands raked along her outer thighs, then moved to the tender inner flesh. She parted willingly for him. His middle finger penetrated her. It was her turn to gasp with delight.

"Not just your finger. This. *This!*"

She jerked hard on his shaft, pulling it toward the spot filled with his finger. Moistness turned to a veritable flood as he continued to stroke in and out, occasionally finding the tiny spire just outside her nether lips so he could press his thumb down on it. She thrashed about as he continued to feel her up.

"So good, John, so good. But I want more."

"What?" he teased. "What more do you want?"

"Your cock!"

Her tugs became too insistent for him to resist. Rolling over, he came to his knees between her parted thighs and looked down at her. Melissa's eyes were half closed and her lips slightly parted. She slowly looked up and then down to his crotch. He felt her insistent pull, drawing him forward to the spot he desired most to fill.

He caught himself on his hands as his hips slid forward. The tip of his stalk touched dewy, trembling lips then parted them to dash far into her. She gasped and lifted her rump off the ground to grind her hips into his.

Slocum remained fully buried in her moist, tight interior until he had to move. Slowly withdrawing until only the purple cap at the end of his manhood remained within her, he gathered his strength and stroked forward. This time he moved smoothly and sank balls deep. Again completely surrounded by gripping female flesh, he paused, reveling in the heat and tightness.

"Faster, do it faster," she moaned. Her fingers gripped his upper arms, fingernails cutting into his flesh.

He began moving with more determination, obeying not only her request for more speed but also his own need. Friction mounted along his entire length, burning at him, tearing away at his control.

Faster. Faster yet. He was on fire. Her knees lifted to either side of his body, giving him an even tighter target to fill with his pulsating manhood. But he could not continue as long as he wanted. Deep inside blossomed a white fire that spread rapidly, burning his loins and then exploding out the tip hidden far inside her.

She clamped a hand over her mouth to stifle her outcry.

She thrashed about, his erection the axle about which she spun. And then she sagged down. Slocum bent down and kissed her. Melissa's eyes opened, and she stared at him.

"As good as I thought," she said in a husky whisper.

"It gets better," he told her.

"Prove it."

After a while, he did.

9

"I need to go, John." Melissa pushed away from him, sat up, and then wiggled delightfully as she worked her skirt down from around her waist, where it had stayed almost all night long. She turned, bent, and kissed him, then reached over and tucked him back into his jeans. "You should button up before you fix breakfast."

With that she was up and hurrying into the darkness. Slocum tried to see what time it was by the position of the stars but clouds had moved in, promising a storm later in the day. He didn't like the notion of being caught on the trail, even if they were on the easy section, in a downpour.

He leaned back, then took her advice, and buttoned up. She didn't want her brother knowing how she had spent the night. Slocum had to agree. Stephen was a nervy fellow and prone to jumping to conclusions. That his sister was with the hired help all night long would set him off and produce either anger or, worse from Slocum's view, surliness. Once they got on the trail, the three of them needed to pull together or they would end up like the first party of prospectors had.

Slocum checked his six-shooter, then pulled out his watch

and peered at the face. The faint illumination showed him it was hardly 4 a.m. He settled back, thinking about how pleasurable—and unexpected—it had been with Melissa during the night. It was possible that everything was looking up for him.

He might even find what happened to her pa. That would benefit them all.

Tossing and turning, he found it impossible to get back to sleep, so he rose, secured his bedroll, and wandered down the incline to make a fire pit. As he worked, he took a deep breath and caught the odor of burning wood on the breeze. When he'd finished gathering wood and had everything ready for a cooking fire, he went exploring.

Less than a hundred yards back along the trail he caught the aromatic scent of freshly brewed coffee. Alert now, he advanced more slowly and finally saw the glow of a fire a few yards off the trail. From what he could tell in the faint glow from the coals, three men huddled about drinking coffee. No words reached him, but the sight of mules secured to a line convinced him they were prospectors on their way over the pass to find fortune in the goldfields.

He retraced his steps, reached the camp, and started his own fire. Stephen was first to come from his post near the mules, grumbling and yawning.

"Coffee? Just boiled some," Slocum said, holding up the coffeepot.

"Yeah," was all he got as a mumbled answer. Stephen found his cup and let Slocum slosh some of the liquid in it. He made a face when he tasted it, then said, "This tastes awful."

"You can make it next time," Slocum said. He took a drink of the bitter coffee and fought to keep from making the same comment. Supplies bought down below were overpriced and only barely drinkable.

"Needs a shot of whiskey in it to cut the taste," Stephen said.

"Of course you brought some, didn't you, dear brother?"

Melissa seated herself next to Stephen across the fire from Slocum. She avoided his eyes, but he saw a tiny smile curling the corners of her bow-shaped lips.

Slocum began fixing some oatmeal, and as he stirred it, he asked, "Would you be willing to throw in with another party going over the pass?"

"Another? Who?" This caught Melissa's attention.

"Three prospectors are on the trail a quarter mile behind us. If we team up, there'd be safety in numbers."

"You make it sound as if we're sheep and there are wolves out there," Stephen scoffed.

"Not far off," Slocum allowed. "I don't know them or if they'd be willing, but I think they would." He stared straight at Melissa. This time she caught his eye and blushed. What red-blooded prospector wouldn't want to share the trail with a woman this lovely?

"It would make the night safer," she said slowly.

He read more into her words than Stephen. With others standing guard, they wouldn't be able to spend the night as they had, but splitting sentry duty made reaching Desolation Pass more likely.

"I want to speak with them. To see how they act. I won't allow ruffians around you, Melly."

"Oh, grow up, Stephen. I can take care of myself. I've heard bad language."

"Because you insisted on going to work with Pa."

"What kind of work did he do?" Slocum asked.

Brother and sister looked at him as if he had grown a second head.

"He's a mining engineer, of course. Why else would he come out here to find gold?" She frowned. "What did you think his occupation to be?"

"Never came up," Slocum said. "I reckoned he was like the others, a man looking for quick wealth." His guess of lawyer had been entirely wrong.

"Oh, no, Papa is a methodical, realistic man. He had seen enough mining to yearn for gold, of course, but if he failed as a prospector, he could hire himself out at a tidy sum to design and oversee a working goldmine."

"What sort of mining did he do?"

"Although he was most familiar with coal mining, he was quite well read in geology. I daresay he could run an assay office, with the proper equipment and chemicals."

Slocum stood and turned to the trail as the three prospectors in the trailing party made their way. They stopped, put their heads together, and argued. From the snippets Slocum overheard, they were discussing what he already had with Melissa and Stephen. He walked over to them, keeping his hands well away from his six-shooter.

"Morning, gents," Slocum called.

They returned his greeting, and in a few minutes they huddled around the fire Slocum had built, drinking coffee and trying not to be too obvious about staring at Melissa. They were successful in draining the coffee; not ogling the lovely woman proved their bane.

"We kin throw in with you. Heard stories of how scavengers pick up equipment tossed off to make the going easier," said the burly prospector Slocum pegged as the leader.

"More than simply picking up discarded equipment," Slocum said. "A gang of road agents will kill everyone in a party and steal their mules and supplies."

More discussion went around the circle, only Melissa holding back from contributing her opinion. The way she looked at him made Slocum feel a bit warm—and tight in the jeans. For two cents, he would have let Stephen come to an agreement with the prospectors so he and Melissa could have more time together in the woods, out of sight.

"Then it's decided. We ride together but keep separate camps. We share guard duty, maybe with some overlap."

Slocum let Stephen seal the deal by spitting on his palm and shaking hands with Atkins, the other party's leader. He almost laughed when he saw Stephen rub his hand in the dirt afterward.

Getting everything lashed onto the mules took longer than he'd expected since Melissa came to help. Every time he reached to tighten a cinch or pull a rope into place across a canvas pack, she stooped slightly and grabbed his crotch. By the time Slocum was finished, he was mighty sore between the legs.

He told her so.

Melissa laughed and said, "Just wait. You'll be plenty sore by the time we reach the pass." She sobered when she realized why they were on the trail, then flashed him a small smile. "We will find him, won't we, John?"

"Won't be from lack of trying."

Stephen called that Atkins and his partners were ready to hit the trail. Slocum took special delight in helping Melissa up. His hand slipped under her skirt and stroked along her leg almost to her nether lips. He jerked free before she dropped hard onto the saddle. Otherwise his hand would have been trapped.

"Serves you right almost breaking your hand," she said. "That was an ungentlemanly thing to do." In a voice even lower she added, "And I want more!"

Slocum swung up onto the mule and got it moving to join the others. Melissa was slower to follow, having trouble getting her balky animal to obey, but she kept at it and soon passed Slocum and her brother to talk with Atkins and the other two.

Stephen came up alongside and spoke, his eyes never leaving the three men and his sister ahead.

"You think she'll be all right with them? They're rough fellows."

"Melissa doesn't have any trouble talking to men, does she?"

"The little tramp," Stephen muttered, thinking Slocum didn't hear. Louder, "She has an active social life."

"I expect so."

By the end of the day they had traversed the long level stretch and were again faced with a steep trail up the mountainside. The six studied the climb ahead.

"You want to scout fer us, Slocum? You said you was good at that kinda thing."

"No need. The trail's well marked. If others have made it through, so can we."

"I'd feel safer if you led the way. You got more experience on these danged mules than any of the rest of us," Atkins said.

"You're doing just fine."

"I'll be right behind." Atkins motioned for his two friends to follow, letting Melissa ride behind them and Stephen bring up the rear.

Slocum urged his mule up. The surefooted beast took the incline easily, dislodging a few rocks as it climbed steadily. For an hour they rode, until they found themselves edging along part of the trail that pressed against the mountain on their right and afforded a fifty-foot drop on the left. This didn't bother Slocum unduly, but he heard the others grumbling.

Slocum turned and stared hard when he heard Atkins say, ". . . better in the town when . . ."

The rest disappeared in a gust of wind, but Slocum thought he heard "true."

Before he could fall back, let Atkins take the lead, and ask, he heard a loud scream. The trail curved around the face of a sheer rock. Seconds later, Melissa cried out, too.

"Stephen, Stephen! Are you all right? Stephen!"

"What happened?"

"Danged if I know," Atkins said. "You want to keep on?"

Melissa didn't stop screaming.

Slocum slid from the mule and edged his way past Atkins and one of his partners. Melissa was behind him and already on the trail, on hands and knees looking over the side.

"John, help him. Stephen fell!"

"Son of a bitch," he muttered. He stepped closer and chanced a look out. The incline here wasn't as sheer as in other places, and that might have saved the man's life. Stephen lay twenty feet below, thrashing about feebly.

"You need a rope or something to go fetch him?" Atkins asked. The man had come back to see what the trouble was. He led Slocum's mule.

"What happened?" Slocum looked from Melissa to Atkins's other partner, who was behind Stephen's mule.

"Can't rightly say," the prospector said. "He was a bit wobbly in the saddle. Might have leaned out, got dizzy like, then taken a fall. Seen it happen before."

"Where?"

"What's that?" The prospector looked up, startled. The expression on his face told the story.

Slocum went for his six-shooter but something struck him in the back and knocked him from the trail. He flailed about, grabbing thin air, then plunged downward to join Stephen Baransky. He landed hard, tried to get up, and found he couldn't. Slocum collapsed, and the world turned to darkness all around him.

10

The moans grew louder, but it took Slocum a few seconds to realize he wasn't the one making the sounds. He stirred and felt jabs of pain throughout his body. He stopped trying to move and worked on recovering his senses a little at a time. The sun was warm on his head so only a few minutes—an hour at most—could have passed. He sucked in a breath and let the wave of pain roll through him. Then he opened his eyes and saw that he was right about the source of the agony.

Stephen Baransky lay in a heap a few yards away. A wound on his face bled. Good. That meant he was still alive since dead men didn't bleed. Slocum pushed out with his hands and found solid rock to support himself. Using this advantage, he sat up. Another minute went by as he examined himself. No bones broken. He had lost some skin when he hit the rough rock and skidded along a few feet, but luck had been with him again.

If he had slipped another couple feet, he would have plunged another fifty. Surviving that fall would have taken more than luck. At the moment, Slocum doubted divine intervention was going to matter a whole lot to him. He had been dry-gulched again, and this caused his blood to boil. Using the anger to focus his strength, he got to his feet and took a few shaky steps toward Stephen.

The young man's eyes fluttered open. A look of pure hatred turned his bloody face into a mask when he recognized Slocum.

"You did this. You're responsible."

"You're the one that took a header over the side. I . . . I don't know what happened to me. I started to get a rope to come down and rescue you and—"

He bit off the words as his last seconds on the trail rushed back.

"Atkins's partner knocked you off your mule."

"I think so. I can't remember. I was up there, and then I was down here. Everything in between is a blur, but it's your fault!"

Slocum wasn't inclined to argue since he agreed. If he hadn't had the bright idea of teaming up with the other party, they wouldn't have had a chance to shove him and Stephen over the side of the cliff.

"Melissa!" Slocum stepped away from Stephen and looked to the trail twenty feet over his head. He shouted her name, but the sound bounced off the rock and quickly turned into the soft sound of a wind blowing past jagged rocks. He looked around and saw lead-bellied clouds moving in. The night before he had suspected rain would make their travel miserable. It had held off this long.

"Where is she? Melly! Melly! Where are you?"

Stephen fought to get to his feet, then doubled over as pain hit him in the gut. He fumbled in his side pocket and drew out a flask, tipped it back, and swallowed a hefty slug. The aroma of bourbon reached Slocum. His mouth watered for just a hint of that whiskey, but Stephen didn't offer. He remembered something Melissa had hinted at about her brother. She thought he drank too much, and he thought she slept around.

They were both right.

"We've got to scale that rockslide," Slocum said. "We'd better do it quick."

"What happened to her?"

"Don't worry about her right now. Worry about yourself. We don't want to be caught on bare rock if the sky opens up. A gully washer on the prairie is bad enough. Here it can sweep all the way down the mountainside and take anything without roots with it."

Slocum checked to be sure the leather thong held his six-gun in the holster, then patted his vest pocket to assure himself the watch was intact. His brother's legacy was still ticking.

So was John Slocum. He began climbing, choosing his foot- and handholds carefully and moving at a steady pace. When he had gotten halfway to the trail, Stephen called to him.

"I can't make it. I'll pick the wrong rocks and fall."

"Use the places where I've been."

"But—"

Slocum paid him no further heed. He returned to working his way upward like a human spider. Once the rock gave way under his boot and sent a cascade down onto Stephen's head. The way the young man cursed told Slocum he was making progress and didn't need help. By the time he pulled himself up onto the trail, a heavy raindrop smashed into the crown of his hat. The *splat!* was so loud he thought it was a gunshot. When others followed, he knew they were in for a real frog strangler of a storm.

He crawled across the road and put his back to the side of the mountain and waited for Stephen to join him. It took a few more minutes, and by that time both men were soaked through and through. Slocum had to laugh at how bedraggled Stephen looked. Then he quieted. They were in a fix. Atkins and the other two prospectors—if they even were prospectors and not road agents—had their mules.

"Where's Melly?"

"She must have been taken prisoner," Slocum said, knowing what that meant. He forced himself to his feet and pulled the brim of his hat down to shield his eyes from the rain. He started walking back in the direction they had ridden.

"Where are you going?"

"To find your sister. And our mules." He pulled his coat around so it protected his Colt from the driving rain.

"How'll you find her?"

Stephen half walked, half stumbled to catch up with Slocum's long stride.

"There's no way to track them in this rain. Five minutes would erase any trail."

Slocum hardened inside. "That doesn't much matter because there are only two ways they could have gone."

"Why not keep going?"

"Not up the mountain to the pass. That's harder than going downhill." Slocum didn't add that he had overheard one of the scavengers talking and had caught part of a name. He had to have been talking about Trueheart. That meant the trio was likely to take Melissa to the scavenger's boomtown high in the mountains rather than all the way to Almost There.

At least he hoped that was what would happen. The three might use her, then kill her. For them, that would be striking it rich.

"We could pass them in this downpour and never know it." Stephen struggled to keep up. He pulled the collar of his coat around his neck and lowered his head. The brim of his bowler hardly protected his face from the rain.

"We keep walking," Slocum said. And he did. But even when the rain let up just before sundown, he hadn't overtaken the kidnappers. The torrential rain had erased any possible trail.

Slocum reached into his pocket and drew out the silver dollar with the hole shot through it. This was his ticket back into Trueheart's thriving outlaw hideout. But it wouldn't do to show up at the gate on foot. He needed some reason to enter and couldn't think of anything other than stolen mounts or equipment.

"What are we going to do?"

"We keep walking. All the way back to town."

"I don't have much money."

"I've got some," Slocum said. "What we can't buy, we'll steal."

"But—"

"For Melissa," he said. "For your sister."

"For Melly I'd steal the moon from the night sky," Stephen said with pepper in his voice.

They reached the town at the base of Desolation Mountain just before sundown four days later. Slocum was footsore, and every time he stepped down, he got angrier. He had been robbed and lost three men—and two Baranskys. He wasn't sure which galled him more, not finding Clem or having his daughter spirited away as she had been.

Slocum knew the answer. There would be blood in the streets to rescue Melissa Baransky.

Clem might still be alive, but it was the woman Slocum would kill to save.

"I don't think I can walk another step," Stephen said. He dropped into a chair in front of the saloon, ignoring the blare of music coming from inside. Someone banged hard on the piano, almost coaxing out a recognizable song.

"We can find somewhere to sleep, then outfit ourselves in the morning." Slocum was equally tired from the long hike, but he intended to scout around town before he went to sleep to find any hint that the three prospectors had brought Melissa all the way back here. They would have arrived a day or two earlier.

"I've got almost a hundred dollars," Stephen said. "How much will that buy?"

"Not enough," Slocum said. He had some of the money taken off Gunnison. It wasn't much. "It'll be better if you stay in town and let me get on the trail."

"What trail?" Stephen said bitterly. "The rain wiped out any tracks. You said so yourself. With my own eyes I *saw* how even the main trail was almost obliterated."

Slocum didn't want to mention Trueheart's town up on the far eastern side of the mountain, fearing Stephen might shoot off his mouth in front of the wrong men. He snorted as he considered that there weren't any right men in this godforsaken place. No marshal, no sheriff, there wasn't even a mayor or town council in Almost There. He suspected Trueheart ran this town as surely as he did the one higher on the hill, but there was no point in dwelling on it.

Melissa was gone. Getting her back as fast as he could was all that mattered.

"I go with you, Slocum. You owe us, but she's my sister."

"She accused you of being a drunk, and you called her a trollop."

"So? We're always chewing on each other like a dog does on an old, familiar shoe. We're siblings. Calling each other names is something we've done all our lives."

Some families were like that, but Slocum's hadn't been that way at all. His older brother had taught him to hunt and shoot, and his pa had shown him every trick a farmer needed to bring in a decent crop, no matter what the conditions. His ma had been a good cook and was respected at the church meetings. She had taught Slocum and his brother how to read and write. There had been some arguments among them, but his pa had always set them straight.

Most of all, Slocum and his brother were inseparable, standing up for each other against all comers.

He touched the pocket watch and missed Robert anew. He had died during the senseless Pickett's Charge and had never lived to see much beyond the Slocum farm that wasn't battlefield.

"I'll see what mules are in the corral. There's only the one merchant selling them."

"I'll come along," Stephen said, showing as much hard-headedness as any mule.

Rather than argue the point, Slocum went to the merchant's corral and checked the swaybacked beasts of burden penned there. He expected to find the mule that had once belonged to Clem Baransky and which he had bought a second time, but none of these miserable creatures was close to it in appearance.

"They might not have gotten back yet," Stephen said. Then he muttered, "Sorry, not thinking. They were ahead of us on the trail and riding, unless they kept on going. How are we going to find Melissa?"

Slocum didn't want to believe that the scavengers hadn't returned to this town with the stolen mules and supplies, but it didn't seem so. That meant they had gone directly to True-heart's hideout. He hadn't shared that knowledge with Stephen because he didn't want to deal with the young man insisting on an all-out attack to rescue his sister. Getting into the town would require using the plugged silver dollar again. It wouldn't be hard to fix one for Stephen, but Slocum didn't want to worry about what he might do once in True-heart's stronghold.

And what he said might be right. The prospectors might have pushed on up the trail with Melissa as their prisoner. They could sell her in the goldfields for as much as they could get grubbing in the dirt for gold nuggets.

He didn't share this notion with Stephen either.

"We should look around town for her," Slocum said. "You want to start at the far end and work toward the center and I'll do the same from the west side?"

"Splitting up will cut the time finding her in half," Stephen said, nodding. "How do you let me know if you find her?"

"There might be gunplay." Slocum eyed the way Stephen pressed his hand into a pocket. He might have a hideout gun there. "We need to keep a low profile, or we will all get put into early graves."

"I won't let those sons of bitches keep her one second longer than necessary."

"Then we need to start hunting for her."

Slocum spoke to thin air. Stephen was already off to hunt building by building for his sister. After an instant of apprehension at what the young man might do, Slocum heaved a sigh of relief at getting rid of him. His gut said that the scavengers—and Melissa—had not returned here. To rescue her he had to get to the center of Trueheart's outlaw empire.

He considered taking one of the mules and riding out, but he needed supplies. All that was locked up in the merchant's store. He started for the back door when he heard two men arguing.

Slocum stepped into shadow and pressed against the store wall as two men passed him less than ten feet away. They never noticed him spying on them.

"Got to get back right away. Going to be a big shipment soon."

"Ah, Mackley, Trueheart's been sayin' that fer a month."

"This time it's for real. Ever since he got that new guy, production's up."

"Why do you think he's gonna cut us in on this? We been with him for six months. You see how he treats everybody."

"That's why we got to stay close."

Slocum edged along the wall and got a view of the two men beside the corral. The man with his back to him was a stranger, but Mackley's ugly face was identifiable in the dim starlight now that he had heard the man named.

"You ain't sayin' we ought to double-cross him, are you? Remember what happened to—"

"You'd prefer him to double-cross *you*? Wise up. If shipments start going out along the new road, there'll be some problems. All I'm sayin' is that we take advantage of them."

"I don't follow. What are you sayin'?"

Mackley let out a hiss that sounded like steam from a locomotive.

"What if a wagon went over the edge of the road?"

"Like that first bend?"

"I was thinking farther down the road, the sharp turn not a mile from the bottom. That's better because we wouldn't have to move the shipment—or what we take out of it—very far."

"You always were a thinker, Mackley."

"With Hersh gone, we need to find somebody else who can get us a wagon. Ain't nobody here in this damned town who can do it."

The two descended into a discussion of whom to trust and whom to double-cross. Slocum waited patiently until the two men led the mules from the corral and disappeared westward.

He had a decision to make. It wasn't hard. Slocum set off after the pair of scavengers, hand resting on the butt of his six-shooter.

11

Slocum hesitated trailing Mackley and his henchman when he heard a gunshot from the main street. When he looked back, Mackley had disappeared. He was torn between going after Mackley and maybe not finding him and sticking like flypaper to the scavenger he still saw. More gunshots spooked the outlaw. He swung onto the back of the decrepit mule and put his heels to its bony flanks. It shot off like a rocket, but Slocum knew it wouldn't keep up that pace long.

He dashed after the departing man and saw him going eastward along the main road into town. As he had thought, the road Trueheart had built to his hidden mountain town came down the far side of the mountain away from Almost There and the trail up to Desolation Pass. Mackley would be going back soon, too, because the shipments were to begin soon. What those might be, Slocum didn't know for certain but had a good idea.

He slowed and finally stopped at the edge of town. Stephen prowled about in the town hunting for his sister. Slocum ought to let him know he was leaving town, but that would create a new row. He had pacified the young man a

96

little by allowing him to begin a search, but Melissa Baransky wasn't in this town.

She was up on the mountainside in Trueheart's. If she was alive at all.

More gunshots sounded, convincing Slocum he shouldn't return and get embroiled in the squabble. Prospectors were like cowboys when it came to letting off steam. They'd fight hugely, drink even more grandly, and then fight again. Afterward, they'd pick up their battered carcasses and return to their backbreaking work. In the case of the prospectors, they were convincing themselves it was worth the danger to crawl over Desolation Pass into a certified gold strike.

Stride long, Slocum started after the man on the mule. The clouds promised more rain. Worse, they kept the night plunged into almost total darkness, but Slocum didn't track by sight alone. At night it was easy to miss visual clues that would be immediately obvious in the light of day. Instead, he kept sniffing the air and listening hard for sounds ahead. The only one on the road at this time of night would be his quarry.

For a half hour he walked at a pace that had to match, if not surpass, that of the scrawny mule. But it was his keen hearing that alerted him to rocks tumbling and the mule wheezing somewhere off the road to his left. Backtracking, he moved slowly until he found a spot where more than a mule or two had left the main road.

Wagons had come this way, cutting into the embankment. The heavy rain had wiped out all wagon wheel imprints, but this worked in his favor now. He found fresh tracks in the mud leading up into the hills on the eastern slope of Desolation Mountain.

Within a hundred yards of hiking uphill, he found himself on a roadbed in better condition than the main road into town. It sloped upward, was broad, and best of all, carried one set of tracks about right if left by a mule.

He doubted the rider ahead could leave the road—there

was nowhere to go other than up. The trail on the western slope of the mountain showed many branches because of the prospectors hunting spots for an easier climb and even because of the scavengers coming from Trueheart's stronghold in such numbers. But here? There was one road and one alone.

Slocum puffed and panted when the road turned even steeper. He wondered how a loaded wagon could ever make it up this grade, even with a team of six or eight mules pulling.

"Oxen," he gasped out as he kept walking. "Might be the teams are oxen."

He hadn't seen any of the animals in Trueheart's town but there hadn't been that much time to look around, and he certainly hadn't been looking for oxen.

A sudden bend in the road made him stop and look over the verge. A slow smile came to his lips. This had to be the place where Mackley intended to dump the contents of a shipment, then pick and choose what to leave to be stolen from Trueheart later. It was a good spot. The sharp bend in the road provided a reason for a spill. Let a driver misjudge by an inch and over the wagon would go. With the grade this steep, brakes had to be applied constantly. An inexperienced freighter might be hard-pressed to brake, keep control of his team, and have the wheels remain on the road.

A braying caught his attention. The sound came from above where the road switched back at a sharp angle. The outlaw wasn't too far ahead of him.

Feet hurting from too much walking, Slocum decided he could ride the rest of the way, if not in style then on a sway-backed mule. He gritted his teeth and plunged ahead along the road, found the cutback, and saw the mule and its rider ahead. The mule had balked at an even steeper grade and the rider thought to get it to move by whipping it.

This made the mule dig in its hooves and rock back on its rump, causing the man to slide back.

"You damned bag of bones. Get to your feet. I—"

He got no farther. Slocum didn't try to hide his advance. The rattle of stones under his boot soles alerted the rider.

"It's me—Mackley," Slocum called out. In the dark it was impossible to make out details.

"You ain't Mackley. You'd—"

The man went for his six-shooter too late. Slocum fired first. He knew he hadn't made a killing shot and didn't want to. He needed information he could never get from a corpse.

"You son of a—" The scavenger stepped back, twisted about, and fired into the air. Slocum started to add a second slug to the first one but he no longer had a target. The man had disappeared over the edge of the road.

Cautiously advancing, Slocum peered over the edge and saw the man's body smashed onto rocks below. From the crazy bend to his body, he wasn't likely to have survived the fall.

Slocum slid his six-gun back into his holster, feeling cheated. He could have gotten information from the man about not only Trueheart's mysterious shipment but the town and probably even Melissa Baransky. The road was new and led to the back of Trueheart's town. Did it require a different ticket to enter? Slocum touched the plugged silver dollar and figured this was still good to get him past the guards.

And now he could ride in style.

It took a few minutes of coaxing, but he convinced the mule to stand and then take his weight. Because he wasn't in a hurry and let the mule pick its own way, travel went smoothly if not quickly. Several hours later, after the sun had popped above the horizon and was immediately eaten by heavy clouds, he saw another steep drop-off at the edge of the road. This had to be the other spot considered for tipping over Trueheart's wagon. Slocum had to admire Mackley's skill in planning. The other turn in the road gave better access to whatever cargo was allowed to remain on the ground.

The mule diligently walked, and Slocum did nothing to

hurry it along. He constantly looked down at the road, expecting to see Mackley making his way up, but the road remained deserted. From what he could tell, the dead out-law's body wasn't likely to be seen by a rider coming from the lower elevations. Even a rider descending would have to know where to look to see it. This gave Slocum some hope he could escape detection.

After sundown he saw a signal fire burning ahead. He had considered stopping for the night, but the mule seemed content to keep walking and time crushed down on top of him. Melissa had been taken three days earlier. How long she would survive as Trueheart's prisoner—if she had even been taken to him—gave a concern that wore down on Slocum.

The fire neared and finally Slocum stopped a few yards away. Two guards with rifles carried easily in the crooks of their arms came out from under a lean-to. They expected no trouble, and Slocum intended to give them none if they let him pass.

He took out the silver dollar with the hole through it, held it to his eye, and watched the pair approach.

"Mind if I see it?"

Slocum flipped the coin to the guard, who caught it and deftly slipped it between thumb and forefinger. He held it high, scrutinized it, then tossed it back.

"Yup, right year and everything."

Slocum caught his breath. He had never considered that only specific years as noted by the mint mark would be acceptable. He thanked his lucky stars that he hadn't allowed Stephen to bull his way along and try to pass a silver dollar with the wrong year stamped onto it. Trueheart was sneakier than he had thought.

"Go on in. There's a new singer at the saloon. Heard tell she's quite a looker . . . and she don't wear nuthin' under her skirt!"

The men laughed. Slocum joined in, but his heart almost

stopped beating. It felt as if cold fingers had closed around its throbbing life.

"What's she look like?" The words came out strong, but Slocum felt as if he had fallen off the side of the mountain as he asked.

"Don't matter. Don't matter she can't sing a lick either. All she has to do is bounce around and hike them skirts." The men laughed again. Slocum knew he wasn't likely to find out more than he already had. He put his heels to the mule and was surprised when it shot forward past the watch fire and took a fork in the road leading away from the main street.

Slocum tried to steer the mule back toward the saloon, but it wasn't having any of that. He gave up trying because he didn't want the mule to balk on him as it had the previous rider. Somehow the mule had taken it into its head to go this way and no other.

He soon found the reason. As he rounded a bend, a large corral filled with a dozen or more mules stretched before him. The mule went directly for the watering trough. Slocum kicked his leg over the mule's back and landed hard. His legs almost gave way since he had been in the saddle so long.

"You want to put that sorry excuse for a mule into the corral?"

Slocum half turned, hand going to his gun. He took his hand away and faced a portly man with muttonchops and the look of a farmer about him.

"You feed all the animals?"

"Some of the human ones, too. You don't look in such bad condition that you need my services."

"Go on and sprinkle some feed out. It's a long way up the mountain," Slocum said. He started to pull money from his pocket, but the man didn't ask for any. With a hard tug he got the mule away from the water and then followed it to the feed. "You have the mule ready to ride by morning?"

"You partial to this one?" The man looked surprised. "Hell, you can take any of 'em in the corral. This one's real mean lookin'."

"He never quits moving. I like that."

"Won't matter much longer since Trueheart's gonna make us all rich. You kin buy yourself a racehorse then."

"Maybe two," Slocum said. He wanted to find out more about Trueheart's scheme, but he needed to find Melissa.

"Guards out on the road said there was a new singer."

"Rich and Henry out there? Yeah, they'd like the new chanteuse, but chances are they never heard a note."

"Skirts," Slocum said. This provoked deep laughter that made the man clutch his sides.

"Yup, you got it."

"Fiery redhead from their description."

"Dang, those boys have gone plumb blind. She ain't no redhead. She's got what my mama used to call chestnut hair. Carries it in a ponytail so's all the better to know what yer ridin'!"

He laughed again, but Slocum had heard enough.

Steps leading down toward town provided a quicker way to the saloon than retracing the road. As before, Slocum found himself caught up in a morass of men, only now he was caught in a tide going toward the saloon. From his vantage point a hundred yards off, he heard a piano banging out a tune and the roar of dozens of men drowning out any possible hint as to the singer's identity. But Slocum knew. Who else could it be?

He let himself be buffeted around like a leaf caught in a tornado and finally squeezed his way into the crowded saloon. A quick look around failed to reveal Melissa, but the stage at the far end of the long room had tattered curtains drawn. The piano player gamely tried to keep the crowd interested, but there was no question what they all wanted.

"Bring her on!"

"Take it off!" shouted another drunk patron crushed against the bar.

"Pass 'er 'round!"

"After she sings," protested a man who might have been the saloon owner. He stood to one side of the stage and looked both fearful and greedy at the same time. Whatever his expression, he wasn't acting.

Slocum moved to a spot in the corner where he got a decent view of the stage. He tried to figure out what he would do. There was no doubt this crowd couldn't be fought. Anyone trying to take away their star performer would be ripped to shreds and stomped into the grimy sawdust on the floor. As much as he hated to admit it, he would have to let the crowd do their worst and try to rescue Melissa afterward.

Afterward.

He began feeling his anger rising as the men shouted increasingly lewd suggestions. Worse, he heard others saying that this was nothing compared to what she had done in earlier shows.

The piano fell silent. Slocum stood a little straighter. Then the piano player began hammering out as loud as he could a song Slocum almost recognized. He didn't try to figure out what he was listening to because the audience fell silent.

When the curtain pulled back, an ear-shattering roar went up. The performer came out, turned, and flashed her bare buttocks at the crowd to great approval. Then she turned and began singing.

It wasn't Melissa Baransky.

12

Slocum lost sight of the woman on stage as the men waved their hats about and hopped up and down to get a better look at her intimate regions. He pushed one man away, got a sour look, then found himself in possession of a chair. Stepping up gave him a better look at the stage. The woman teased, dancing to the edge and throwing her skirt out for the benefit of those pressed close to the stage. The man who had introduced the act came by, charging for a look and even more for a fleeting touch.

Different negotiations went on when the men tired of just watching and groping. How much was charged Slocum didn't know, but the performance became more active, with the crowd shoving wads of money at the man to take their turn with the woman on stage.

Slocum hopped down. He didn't have to watch. Pushing his way to the saloon door, he bumped into the man who had taken care of his mule.

"Really somethin', ain't it?" the man said.

"I'm not much for watching," Slocum said.

"Me neither. That's why I go over to Sally's. She got

herself a new girl what looks a bit like that one, only purtier. Nice brown hair, too. That's what I like, though on occasion a palomino ain't amiss."

"Another girl?"

"Just the last day or two. Usually news like that goes fast around this town, but things have been hoppin'. That's kept most of the men busy."

"It can do that," Slocum said. He was torn between asking about the newcomer at the cathouse and finding what went on in Trueheart's town.

"You headin' fer Sally's? That's where I'm goin'."

"You tried this new girl?"

"Cain't afford her. Sally knows a good thing when she sees it. Don't know where she come from—out on the trail, I suspect, but what a looker like her was doin' headin' for the goldfields is beyond me."

"She might make a pretty penny there."

"She could marry herself a rich man, she's so good lookin'. Why bother spreadin' fer a dozen men a day when you kin do it for one and get all the comforts of home?"

Slocum walked alongside as they wove through narrow alleys and finally came to a three-story building not far from Trueheart's big warehouse. A single blue light burned in the downstairs window, but all the windows on the upper floors were bright with oil lamplight.

"Might be she's not doing this on her own," Slocum said.

"Hell, what whore does? Most are dope addicts and drunks. And those are the least diseased of 'em. One of these days my pecker's gonna fall off from some pox I got pokin' them, but 'til then, I'm not askin' too many questions."

He stopped outside the door and yelled, "Hey, Sally. You got payin' customers. You don't want us to stay outside with our peckers hangin' out. The night air's not good for us."

"Ross, you old reprobate, get yourself in here. Bring your pecker with you."

"She doesn't mean you," Ross said, laughing as he let the middle-aged woman pull him inside.

Slocum trailed the other man and looked around. Most brothels had a bouncer, but he didn't see one here. The madam might be packing a six-shooter under her voluminous skirts, but he couldn't tell. The sitting room was dimly lit by the blue light in the window. From the head of the stairs gushed bright light and sounds of pleasure.

"Haven't seen you here before. You're welcome, if Ross here vouches for you."

"This here place is by invitation only," Ross explained.

"Him and me got the same taste in ladies, Sally. He just rode in, but he looks like a gentleman."

"Are you a gentleman with money?"

Slocum silently drew out what money he had, then tucked it back into his pocket before Sally could grab it from him.

"I'd like to look over the merchandise," he said.

"This place isn't like the Nubile Nugget, what with their peep show and all."

"That's the saloon," Ross needlessly told him.

"It's Trueheart's own special place, and we're under his protection," the madam went on. "I say the word and Trueheart takes care of any problem. *Any* problem," she emphasized.

"Understood. Now can I see your girls? Ross said you had a new one that might just be what I'm in the mood for tonight."

"She's a special one," Sally said, going up the steep stairs. She made sure Ross and Slocum got a good view of her rump and the bustle bobbing on it. At the head of the stairs she held out her hand for Ross. He was obviously well thought of here.

Slocum reached the top of the stairs and found it opened onto a small sitting area. Three demimondaines lounged on chairs, trying to look demure. None of them was Melissa Baransky.

"These are mighty pretty but . . ." Slocum began.

"But not what you were looking for, eh? She's not here," said Ross. "Why don't you fetch her, Sally? I'd like to look. Just look since I don't have the price."

"She's a princess, a lovely lady the like of which you don't find on the frontier," the madam said, spinning her sales pitch. She made a gesture, and one of the women made a sour face, stood, and went down a hallway toward the back of the house.

Slocum's heart almost exploded when he saw the woman return. With Melissa.

She walked with her head down, only looking up when the madam put a finger under her chin and lifted. Then brown eyes went wide in surprise. She started to speak but Sally cut her off.

"She's a *rara avis*," she said. "That's foreign for rare bird."

"I see that. She's the one I want," Slocum said.

"Of course you do, sweetie," Sally said, "but it'll cost you."

Slocum passed over his greenbacks, but the madam riffled through and shook her head.

"Not enough."

Slocum considered going for his six-shooter then. Ross wasn't armed that he could see, and nowhere had he seen a bouncer to stop him. The threat of Trueheart's anger was enough to stop most men in town. He wondered how well that worked with drunks.

"But I can see that she fancies you, sweetie," Sally went on smoothly. "That's not the way it's been. She's a real hellion when she don't get what she wants."

Melissa held out her arms so Slocum could see the rope burns.

"You tie her down?"

"She likes that," the madam said. "I know it won't be that way with you, unless she asks for it, of course." She cut off any reply from Melissa with a quick, hot look.

"Then we have a deal?"

"Not exactly," Sally said. "You don't have enough by half for a beauty like her."

Slocum said nothing. She was getting to her point in a roundabout way he didn't like.

"You and her, out here on the sofa."

Melissa gasped and said, "Not again! No, I—"

"Quiet, dearie." Sally turned to Slocum. "You get her out here where anyone who pays the fee can watch."

"Anyone?" Slocum asked, considering the use of his six-gun again.

"There were ten before," Melissa blurted. "It was awful."

"I hope you're moving to drop the gun belt, sweetie, because if it's anything else, you're a dead man. That'd be a real shame, too."

Slocum saw that Ross had backed to one wall. Over his head through loopholes poked two rifle barrels that slowly moved to keep Slocum in their sights. From the far wall stuck a third rifle. The bouncers weren't obvious but hid out in passages behind the walls.

"They watch everything," Melissa said. "Even in the rooms."

"You can be gagged," Sally said coldly. "That'd be a pity since the audience likes to hear your cries of pure joy. And she does make them, I assure you. She's going to enjoy you a whole lot." Sally moved to Slocum and ran her fingers under the gun belt and pulled it away.

Slocum saw no way of getting out from under the guns trained on him. If they opened fire, it was likely they would hit Melissa, too. She stared at him with eyes wide, then she nodded slowly and mouthed, "It's all right, John."

He hoped she wouldn't blurt out his name. That was sure to get him killed right away and to doom her to slavery in the whorehouse.

"You look like a stud who can pleasure a woman," Melissa

said. Her words were forced but she had told him she understood their predicament. "What do you have in mind?"

"Do I get to choose?" Slocum asked. He saw that Ross had disappeared and wondered if the man worked for Sally also. It might not have been a coincidence that he steered Slocum in this direction—but it was lucky.

If having a dozen men watching him with Melissa could be considered lucky for either of them.

"Go on, dearie. Strip off that robe of yours. Get naked."

"Let me do it," Slocum said when Melissa reached up to unfasten the sash holding the robe shut.

"You're going to get your money's worth, aren't you? Most of these cowboys just want in and out. The miners are even worse."

"A lot of miners?" Slocum asked. Melissa nodded once, her eyes never leaving his.

He turned when he heard a stampede coming up the stairs. Ross had rounded up eight men, some drunker than lords, others on their way. All clutched scrip in their hands.

"Ten dollars each, gents. Step up, don't crowd. Give this bucking bronco room to perform for you."

"She's purty," whispered one man. "Never seen a filly what looked that good."

This was greeted with cheers and jeers. The crowd wanted to see more. Slocum let them circle around, cutting off a clean shot from any of the riflemen. If he gave them a good enough show—if Melissa went along with him—they would continue to provide cover for whatever he did.

"Strip her down, mister. Git her nekkid!"

Melissa stepped forward, closed her eyes, and took a deep breath. He reached out and ran his fingers down the lapels of the robe, drawing it open to reveal creamy flesh. Slocum tried not to gawk but couldn't help himself. When they had been together before, she had remained dressed. This was the first time he had seen her considerable charms.

Her naked, lovely charms.

He pulled off the sash and carefully laid it to one side, then pushed back the robe off her shoulders. The silk robe fell to the ground, leaving her bare to the waist. Her firm breasts trembled as he cupped them, weighed them like melons, then squeezed down until he elicited a soft moan from her and a loud cheer from their audience.

Stepping closer, he pulled her to him and kissed her. She fought for a moment, then melted into his arms and returned the kiss. He worked from her lips to her ear and whispered, "I don't want to do it like this, but there's no other way."

"The gunmen, I know," she said as she kissed his neck and ear. "They're killers. Killed one man since I've been here."

He ran his hands around her bare back, traced out each bone in her spine, and then worked lower. He cupped the firm, round buttocks and pulled her even harder against him. In spite of the situation, Slocum felt himself getting harder by the instant. She was a beautiful woman and he wasn't able to restrain himself, no matter the situation.

With deliberate moves, he pulled up the frilly undergarment hiding her lower body. With every inch he got new cries of encouragement from the crowd. The roar was deafening when Melissa grabbed the cloth and ripped it off.

"Do it, mister, do it!"

He pressed her back onto the sofa. She dropped to the edge, then reached out and began unfastening the buttons on his fly. When his hardness exploded outward, she took him in her mouth. The road of blood rushing in his ears drowned out the encouragement from the crowd. Slocum was in a world separate from them and shared only by Melissa.

She worked his jeans down as she continued to work her mouth all over him. The tip of his manhood felt as if it was dipped in acid every time her tongue flicked out and touched it before raking along the sensitive underside.

Then she was leaning back on the sofa, knees parted, open for him.

He dropped onto her and wanted to tell her everything would be all right, but the words wouldn't come because it might be a lie if he said that. But what he knew was that he wanted her. In spite of the circumstances, he wanted her.

He moved forward between her spread thighs. She reached down and caught his shaft and guided it to her pinkly scalloped nether lips. The heat and wetness boiling from within took away the last of his inhibitions. He sank into her, an inch at first, then deeper, much deeper.

She gasped. Or was that the watching crowd? He withdrew so that only the head of his manhood remained within her. Then he stroked back in. She arched up off the sofa and ground her crotch to his with every inward thrust. She gasped and sobbed as he withdrew, only to cry out in true desire as he entered her again and again.

The watching men began chanting, and Slocum unconsciously fell into the rhythm of their roar. Deeper, harder, he moved with all the passion locked within his body. And he released Melissa's before he exploded within her. Locked together, they continued to move even after Slocum started to fade.

"Keep them occupied," he whispered in her ear.

She gasped and thrashed about, exposing herself wantonly to draw everyone's attention. Slocum backed away, took up the silk sash he had placed within easy reach, and then spun about, using it like a lasso. The loop dropped around Sally's neck and tightened.

"Call off the men with the rifles," he grated. "Do it or I'll snap your neck."

"You won't get away with this," she said. Any further threat was lost in a gurgle as Slocum tightened the silken noose around her neck. He released it when she began to turn red in the face. "Go on, get out. Show's over."

"The riflemen, too."

"All of you. Take a break. Go on."

Ross herded the audience out, then came over with the bills he had taken from them.

"You put on a real good show, mister." He handed the greenbacks to Sally. "I'll be back for my pay." The man sighed and looked at the naked Melissa sprawled back on the sofa, her legs still spread to keep attention away from Slocum. "Wish I could get a piece of that, but I know I'll have to be satisfied with Roxanne or Mara."

Sally waved him off. Slocum released a bit of the pressure around her neck.

"Get dressed. Really dressed," he said to Melissa. "We're clearing out of here."

"Trueheart will kill you. He's part Sioux. He'll cut your damned heart out and eat it!"

"I don't know where the clothes are kept."

Slocum tightened the sash and forced Sally to point out the wardrobe where the soiled doves' clothing was stored. He watched as Melissa dressed, wishing he could have her again. This had been terrible—and it had been good at the same time. She was lovely and knew how to keep both of them alive, no matter what it took.

"He won't rest until you're dead and he hands her over to every damned miner in this town," Sally went on. "She'll die and it won't be pretty. But you, he'll let you live until you beg for death."

"And then he'll eat my heart," Slocum said sarcastically. He jerked on the sash and pulled her along to the first room. A frightened Cyprian huddled in one corner. She bolted when Slocum motioned for her to leave.

He shoved Sally facedown on the bed and quickly tied her with ropes already fastened to the brass bedstead.

"What are we going to do, John?" Melissa pressed close behind him.

"I should have known you knew her. You're both gonna die!"

He secured the silk sash around Sally's mouth, gagging her. She continued to kick and make a fuss. When Melissa handed him his gun belt, he considered buffaloing the madam.

"No need. The girls have all hightailed it," Melissa said. "I told them she was giving them to Trueheart. That scared the daylights out of them."

This caused Sally to jerk about and struggle even more. Trueheart was likely to blame her for the defection.

"That ought to keep everyone in town occupied for a while."

"Do we—"

He pushed her from the room and closed the door to keep Sally from overhearing his escape plan.

Whatever it might be.

"There's a corral up on the side of the hill. We get to it, we can scare off the mules and horses and get a head start down the back road."

"Back road?"

"You'll find out. Right now we have to hurry before word gets out."

Slocum swung Melissa around to his left side when she tried to cling to his right arm. She gripped him tightly and cried, her hot tears soaked up by his coat.

"It was terrible, John. You can never know."

He could imagine. He had seen every form of torture as he roamed the West. The Apache and Navajo weren't the only ones capable of intense cruelty.

He drew his six-shooter and went down the stairs ahead of her. The lower level was deserted. He opened the door and stepped onto the porch lit by the blue light in the window.

"Come on. Looks like we're in the clear."

He hoped it stayed that way. In any shoot-out, he could only lose. He wanted to take back streets, but first he had to get around Trueheart's huge warehouse.

"This way," he said, choosing to be bold and walk past it as if they belonged, but Melissa stood stock-still. "I said, come on. What's wrong?"

"There. Look, John. Look there!"

He saw three men come from Trueheart's headquarters. He didn't know two of them. The third was Melissa's father.

Clem Baransky was alive and Trueheart's prisoner.

13

"Papa!"

Slocum grabbed her arm and stopped her from attracting the attention of Clem Baransky's guards. The men stood close on either side, herding him as they might a calf to branding. All they needed to make the picture exact was a lasso and a branding iron. From the way Baransky shuffled along, he had already been branded and didn't like it.

"Let go!" Melissa yanked hard, but Slocum held on tight enough to keep her from doing anything foolish.

"They'll kill you and your pa," Slocum said harshly. "We've got to get out of town before she gets loose." He tilted his head back in the direction of the brothel, though Melissa had to know whom he meant.

"I went through hell to find him. I'm not about to let him slip away now." She jerked, again trying to get free.

"Then use your head. We need a way to rescue him and not get killed ourselves. Trueheart has some scheme that he wanted your pa for. His men killed the other three in the party of prospectors I was leading over the pass. Why would Trueheart keep your pa alive?"

"He wanted to make a fortune in the goldfields just like all the others," she said. Her eyes fixed on her father. The two guards moved him away from the warehouse. Slocum relaxed his grip enough to let Melissa go in the same direction, but not fast enough to overtake them. They ran a big enough risk being seen. If Ross happened upon them, all hell would be out for lunch.

Even worse would happen when Sally freed herself.

"Trueheart must have found out that he wasn't just another prospector."

"He has a family. Mama died. That's why he came out here, to get enough money to take her to Europe. There is a surgeon there who can—who could—oh, damn! They've disappeared!"

Slocum eased his grip even more on her and hurried along to the corner of the building. Melissa almost bolted when she saw her pa and Trueheart's men a couple blocks away, still walking, not bothering to hurry. If they didn't mount up and ride away, Slocum knew they would be easily followed. The danger lay in being spotted by some woman-hungry miner who'd draw attention to them because he spotted Melissa.

"Pull up your coat collar," Slocum said. "Hide your face as much as you can. And pull down your hat."

She protested when he yanked it down over her ears. It wasn't stylish, but it hid her long hair. From a distance no one would confuse Melissa with a man, but all Slocum wanted was to hide her lovely face. She might have only been in town a few days, but he suspected she was as notorious in her way as the dancer at the Nubile Nugget Saloon. Sally would be discreet in advertising the newcomer to her brothel to get the most she could for her, at least initially. Slocum had found out firsthand how that could be done. From the way Melissa had acted, this wasn't the first public performance she had been forced into.

"Your ma died," Slocum said harshly.

"But Papa didn't know that. Our doctor in Philadelphia said she would linger for months, but she up and died right after Papa left."

"Why did a gentleman from Philadelphia think he could make money in the goldfields?" Slocum knew the answer. The lure of gold was an addictive drug. Simply thinking about the gold piling up, being pulled from the ground by double handfuls, built on itself until it seemed a certainty. Others got rich. So why not me?

"He's not the gentleman you think," she said, pulling Slocum along now. He let her as he kept an eye peeled for any trouble brewing. So far, Trueheart's men took Baransky through deserted back ways.

"He needed me to guide him and provide along the trail."

"Oh, he's not *that* kind. He's an engineer. He worked in the coal mines throughout Pennsylvania. When the Welsh miners came over, he made a special point of learning all he could from them to add to his college education. He made ever so much money for the mine owners by finding the most profitable veins and the best, cheapest ways of extracting the coal."

"You said he was a geologist."

"He knows minerals. All kinds. With his skill, he was certain to find gold."

"And if he didn't, he could hire out to prospectors who had already struck it rich. There isn't a mine in these parts that doesn't have to be blasted and tunneled."

"He's quite expert with explosives," she said. She stopped and pointed. "What are we going to do?"

Slocum hunted for an answer. The two guards loaded Baransky into the rear of a buggy while both of them climbed onto the driver's seat. As the carriage lurched away, Baransky looked up and saw Melissa. He sat upright and waved.

"His hands are tied!"

"Shackled," Slocum said, but how he was bound didn't

matter. Slocum swung his arm around Melissa's waist and slammed her against the wall of a shop fronting on the main street. She tried to look around him, but he kept his body interposed. After she stopped fighting him, he chanced a look. The guards hadn't noticed Baransky's reaction and drove away without so much as a look back.

"They're taking him away!"

"Must be some distance or they'd've walked," Slocum said, running over everything he knew in his head. "Why would they bother bringing him into town when the mine he's working is somewhere in the hills to the east of here?"

"I don't know, John. We have to get him before they take him into the mine. We'd never be able to rescue him then."

What she said was true, but Slocum still thought on the reason to bring him into town. Into the warehouse.

"Supplies. He was pointing out what he needed to extend the mineshaft."

"Who cares?"

"We can't follow him directly, but whatever he wanted has to be shipped over. It'll be in a heavy freight wagon."

"And we can follow the wagon and rescue Papa!" Melissa threw her arms around his neck and gave him a big kiss. "You're wonderful!"

"We're not out of this mess by a long shot," he said. Slocum's mind raced as he tried to decide what the best plan might be. He was methodical and had proven that repeatedly during the war when, as a sniper for the CSA, he would sit in the crook of a tree for long hours waiting for a single shot at a Federal officer. A flash of sunlight off gold braid, even at several hundred yards, his careful shot, the enemy lacked a commander. More than one battle had turned in the Rebs' direction because of Slocum's accuracy and patience.

But patience was not always a virtue when decisions had to be made quick—and right.

"Ross will bring up a team from the town corral, maybe mules or oxen, depending on how heavy the freight is." He kept Melissa in his arms as he slowly turned in a full circle to better get an idea what was possible and what wasn't.

"Up on the roof of the warehouse," he said. "The freighter will bring the wagon around, probably to that door, where the supplies will be loaded. Then we drop down into the wagon bed."

"We kill the driver and—"

"We try not to be seen."

"I want them all dead!"

"Not until the driver takes us to the mine and your pa."

"Oh," she said in a small voice. "I'm not good at thinking these things through."

"Plan on how you'll get even with Sally and Atkins."

"Atkins," she said, turning the name into a snake's hiss. "I had forgotten about him. He sold me to her! He's no better than a Southern slave owner. He—"

"Hush," Slocum said, pulling her into shadows. He heard mules coming, their braying carrying through the mountain air and even drowning out the jeers and shouts from the saloon. From the noise the miners produced, the bare-assed hootchy-cootchy dancer had begun a new performance.

Slocum looked at Melissa and was thankful, as awful as her ordeal had been, it wasn't nearly as bad as the woman on stage at the Nubile Nugget. It didn't matter if that woman wanted to be there. The man taking up the collection kept the money she earned by exposing her and offering her to a long line of miners. Long after she was worn out or dead, her manager would be spending the money she had garnered.

"We have to hurry. If those mules are pulling a wagon—"

"They are. Listen hard." Slocum heard the clanking of harness and the creaks of a wagon that had carried one load too many.

"We have to get onto the roof! We have to if we're going to jump down."

"Too dangerous now," he said softly. "Just wait. Our chance will come. When it does, we have to be ready."

She tried to protest, but he silenced her with a kiss. She fought him for a moment, then succumbed.

"You know how to get my attention," she said, giggling. Then she sobered as Ross drove past in a heavy wagon, six mules hitched to it.

"We couldn't get onto the roof to jump off. We may not have to," he said.

"Do you think he'll notice if we slip into the back of the wagon once he gets rolling?" Her brown eyes glowed in the dark as she stared up into his face. Slocum felt a pang of consternation. Her pa had trusted him, and it had landed him in Trueheart's clutches. So far, he hadn't done too much better with her and her brother.

"We can only try."

Slocum held her close as Ross and three from inside the warehouse moved tools and tossed them into the back of the wagon. Then came the reason such a wagon had been sent. Case after case was moved, the workers carrying their loads gingerly.

"Dynamite," she said softly.

Slocum had no fear of the explosive. He had worked with it enough to know its limitations and dangers. What worried him were the blasting caps. The fulminate of mercury caps could blow at the slightest touch. A fuse would set them off or a hammer blow or just looking cross-eyed at them.

"Get it secured," Ross said. "Trueheart wants everything to be ready for the morning shift."

"We that close?"

"Who knows? He don't confide much in me. All I know for sure is that I got to get back to feed the mules up in the corral."

"You and your animals."

"I deal with you, don't I?" Ross laughed. It took a few seconds before the others joined in.

"What if they watch him go? What'll we do then?" Melissa sounded less afraid than she did excited. The thrill of danger brought color to her cheeks, and she trembled like a racehorse waiting for the starter's gun.

"Begin walking," Slocum said. The workmen stood in the warehouse doorway as Ross pulled out in the wagon. The mules protested loudly, braying and trying to kick. The driver proved adept enough to both calm them and get the team pulling in unison.

"What?"

Slocum took Melissa's arm and started her on a course parallel to the wagon. As it rattled past, he shoved her to get her into the wagon bed.

The rough ride proved lucky for them. Melissa stumbled and almost fell, but the twisting of the wagon covered the sound of her jumping up onto it. Slocum quickly followed, turned, and sat with his legs dangling over the edge so he could stare back at the warehouse. If the trio that had loaded the wagon noticed the additional riders, they didn't make a fuss over it. Slocum saw a tiny orange coal glowing in the dark. One had built a cigarette and smoked, possibly passing it to his partners. They wouldn't be too interested in anything else.

"What do we do now?"

"Get under the tarp," Slocum said, lifting the dusty cloth so Melissa could crawl beneath it. She hesitantly obeyed. Slocum followed and lay close to her.

She giggled again and reached down to put her hand on his crotch.

"This is more fun than I thought it would be."

"Don't get too distracted," he warned.

"Me? You need to take your own advice." She squeezed down harder, and he began to respond. He reached down, caught her slender wrist, and pulled her hand away. Thinking clearly now meant life or death.

"We need to guess when to jump off. We don't want to get too close to wherever the wagon's headed."

"But we might not find my papa!"

"Not so loud," he said. The rattle of the wagon, clank of

the loaded tools, the complaining mules, and the creak of the harness all muffled her words, but her voice was high-pitched enough to catch Ross's attention.

Slocum chanced a look out from under the tarpaulin but couldn't figure out where they were. Ross had driven east but began following the curve of the mountain so, Slocum guessed, they headed north. It hardly mattered, but he needed to know how to get back to the town and steal enough mules to escape. The roadbed the wagon followed might be all he needed to retrace this route, but Trueheart was a crafty bastard and might have guards stationed along the way.

How long they drove, he couldn't say. The motion of the wagon as it hit potholes and rocks kept him from nodding off, but Melissa pressed close and gave him a sense of invulnerability that proved dangerous.

The sudden halt threw Slocum flat. He fought to regain his balance, but the tools shifted and pinned part of the tarp down.

He kicked and slid backward, finding the edge of the wagon. His boots were exposed—and he heard a man growl deep in his throat like a dog waiting to attack.

"What's goin' on, Ross? What you got back here as freight?"

Slocum reached for his pistol as the tarp was yanked off him and Melissa.

14

Slocum didn't fire but kicked out like a mule, both boots hitting the man squarely in the chest. After the *whoosh!* as air rushed from the man's lungs came a thud when he landed flat on his back.

"Go hide," Slocum said to Melissa. "But wait a second while I lead them off."

He surged to his feet, swung his pistol around, and raked the front sight against Ross's cheek. The driver yelped and grabbed to stanch the sudden spew of blood. He fell back and got his feet tangled in the driver's box, going down hard.

Slocum vaulted the side of the wagon and walked away at a slow, deliberate pace, his Colt Navy at his side. This was his only chance to look around to see where he and Melissa had been brought. The mouth of a mine yawned wide and dark. He considered going in, sending a few bullets down the tunnel, then trying to get away. Any armed miner would return fire and create even more confusion, but he didn't have the chance because Ross had regained his balance and fumbled for a rifle. Worse, the man he had knocked flat on his ass gasped like a blacksmith's bellows

123

and made funny gobbling sounds. It would be only seconds before he unlimbered his six-shooter and started firing.

When two armed guards came from the mineshaft, Slocum took his first shot. His bullet went high and brought down a cascade of dust and rock fragments on their heads, momentarily confusing them.

"What the hell's goin' on?" The guard in the lead lifted his rifle and fired in Slocum's direction.

He knew instantly luck still rode with him and not with the man who had discovered him and Melissa in the wagon bed. A shriek of agony went up, quickly followed by a gurgling sound.

"You damn fool, you done shot Gillespie!" Ross levered a round into his rifle, but Slocum wasn't waiting around to become an easy target.

Dodging, ducking, and weaving, he fired a couple more times to draw fire. He didn't have a chance to look back to see if Melissa had gotten free. If she headed for the far side of the road, she could find cover and wait for the fight to be over.

Slocum dived headlong and skidded along the ground, sharp rocks cutting at his belly as bullets kicked up tiny pillars of dust around him. He scrambled to lie flat behind a knee-high rock. It provided almost no cover but giving Melissa the chance to escape mattered more than his safety. A couple snap shots brought more shouts and the sound of men running to join the fight.

He chanced a quick look around the side of the rock to get a better idea of his predicament. It didn't look good. Four more guards ran from the mine. This puzzled him. Why did Trueheart have so many men in the mine, all armed with rifles? A few miners wielding pickaxes made more sense.

The best he could tell, they had driven a long way around Desolation Mountain, coming down into a long, narrow valley like a knife cut into the rock. The pass lay far above and behind him, but where the goldfields lay wasn't anything he could determine. Trueheart's mine lacked most of the signs of a working mine.

No tailings dribbled out the mouth and down the mountainside, yet there were plenty of men in the mine. From all evidence, a considerable number of wagon loads of material had come to the mine. But for what? The dynamite on this trip meant Trueheart was blasting, but to what purpose?

More bullets cut off Slocum's musing. The guards were finally beginning to coordinate their attack.

Time to move.

Slocum got his feet under him, then lurched and sprinted up the slope that would take him to a spot just above. He slipped and fell flat—and this saved him. A half-dozen slugs ripped into the space where his head had been an instant before. Lying still, he waited for the guards to start arguing among themselves over whether he had been hit, then got back to his feet and made his way upward.

Still being alive took them by surprise and allowed him to get a better spot on the hillside. He kept low and worked his way forward to a rocky ledge over the mouth of the mineshaft. The guards were out of position as Slocum looked down, hoping to see that Melissa had gotten away. Where she had gone, he couldn't tell, but he carelessly kept his head poked up like a curious prairie dog too long.

A rifle bullet knocked his hat off and caused him to recoil. More by reflex than intent, he fired until his six-shooter came up empty.

"He got Ross. Son of a bitch killed Ross!"

Slocum took the time to grab his hat and reload, then edged forward again and saw two men dragging Ross's body from the wagon. He started to fire, then sank back to the ground. They hadn't seen him. If he took a couple easy shots, the other guards would know instantly where he hid.

"Search his pockets, see if he's got any money. He owed me."

Like carrion eaters, the guards swarmed around the dead

driver and began rummaging through his pockets to rob
him. Slocum wanted to turn this to his benefit but didn't see
how—until two men came from the mine.

"What's going on?"

"Somebody killed Ross. We got him on the run. He's in
the hills up there somewhere."

The man from the mineshaft spun and stared hard, but
he couldn't see Slocum in the darkness.

"There's dynamite in the wagon. That's mighty dangerous to be shooting off rifles that close to it."

"These yahoos ain't got the sense God gave a goose. You
go check the explosives, Doc."

The man called Doc went to the rear of the wagon and
hoisted the tarp. From the way he stiffened, then stepped
back a half pace, Slocum knew he had seen something unexpected. The tarp rose a bit, and Slocum knew what it was.

Melissa hadn't been able to escape.

He shoved his six-gun into his holster, moved to a spot
just to the right of the opening to the mine's depth, and
grabbed hold of a protruding beam. He swung down and
landed lightly, staying in a low crouch. It was too much to
hope that he could get the drop on the man who had discovered Melissa because the guards had finished rifling through
Ross's pockets.

"Don't move!"

Slocum stood, hands in the air, considering his chances
and how he could best give Melissa a few seconds to run.
To his surprise, he saw Doc lift the tarp in such a way that
he hid the wagon bed, then dropped it.

"Don't shoot him. Hey, lower your rifles!" Doc moved
forward but was shoved back by the man who had come
from the mine with him.

"What're you pullin', Doc?"

"He's with me."

"What the hell do you mean?"

"He rode out with Ross, that's what I mean. He's a powder monkey. I need help setting the charges."

"Nobody came out with Ross," the man said, but enough doubt rode with his words to give Slocum hope.

"I did. When we pulled up, one of them shot Ross." Slocum pointed to the guards who had rifled Ross's pockets.

"What are you goin' on about?"

"If he said it, it's the truth, Plover. He doesn't lie."

"We never shot Ross. Why'd we do that?"

"You robbed him, that's why," Slocum called.

Plover pointed at Slocum and said, "You shut up. I need to figure this out."

"Nothing to figure out," Doc said, moving close so Slocum got a good look at him. After he got a look at Doc's face, he understood everything.

"Baransky hired me. You want me to give back the money, I can't," Slocum said, running a bluff worthy of a high-stakes game. The man Trueheart's henchman had called Doc was the cause of all his trouble.

"He does know your name, Doc," Plover said dubiously.

"Clement Baransky, that's his name, isn't it? I didn't know he was a doctor."

"I'm no doctor. They call me that because I know 'bout everything," Baransky said.

"Shut up, Doc. You, too. What's his name? Wait, don't answer," Plover said sharply. "Whisper it in my ear. And one of you thievin' magpies, you go have him whisper his name in your ear."

Slocum took a deep breath as one of the gunman came over.

"Don't know what's goin' on. You kilt Ross and I want to see you dead."

"You might have been the one that shot him," Slocum said. Then he whispered his name, repeated it, and waited.

The gunman gave him a sour look and went to where Plover stood with his six-shooter drawn.

"You boys kill him if the names don't match."

"What about Baransky?" Slocum called. He played for time so Melissa could get far away. If she was anywhere close and spying, she would rush back and get them all killed.

"We need Doc, but that don't mean we can't put shackles back on him like we did before." The threat meant something to Baransky because he shivered visibly. Plover motioned his partner closer. "What's the name he gave?"

"Slocum. He said his name was Slocum."

Plover slumped a little, then straightened.

"Matches what Doc said. There was no way they coulda arranged this 'less they knew each other before."

"How'd Doc have any time to hire anybody? Me and Aaron never let him out of our sight when we was back in town."

"That's what you think," Baransky said, laughing harshly. "You two left me in the warehouse while you went out to take a snort from that bottle in your hip pocket."

This set off a long argument that ended with Plover kicking the man in the seat of the pants. Glass shattered and the sharp tang of whiskey momentarily filled the air.

"You didn't have no call hiring anybody, Doc," Plover said, dragging his boot back and forth in the dirt to get the whiskey off it. "You need something, you tell me. I'm the foreman, not you."

"You weren't around. Neither were they. I wanted to speed up the work. Slocum here came along, we talked, I liked what I heard."

"I told Ross and he offered me a ride out. Then they shot him down like a rabid dog," Slocum said, enjoying the new round of incrimination this sparked. Plover blamed Aaron and his partner, who insisted they hadn't shot Ross. The argument turned around full circle with them indicting the other guards from the mine.

Baransky gave Slocum a broad wink.

"Shut up, all of you!" Plover fired into the air to get their attention. "The next round goes into somebody's heart. I'd shoot you in the head, but I want to hurt you for causin' this hash."

"You sayin' I don't have no brains, Plover? I don't take that off nobody!"

The man who had carried Slocum's name to the foreman went for his rifle. Plover gunned him down before the barrel came up halfway to its target. The man dropped to his knees, then flopped back and twitched on the ground. Plover put a second and a third bullet into him.

"I've had it with you jackasses." Plover faced down the others, who exchanged looks.

Aaron said, "It was all his doin', Plover."

"Get the wagon unloaded." Plover motioned to Slocum. "You lend a hand, then we'll have a talk." He plucked Slocum's Colt from his holster. Slocum moved an instant too late to stop him. Plover thrust the six-shooter into his belt.

"I'll keep my gun," Slocum said.

"They'll kill you in the mine if they see you with a six-gun," Plover said.

"Won't matter a whit to you, will it?" Slocum pointed out. "Chances are pretty good I'd go back to town and you—and them—won't get the benefit of my knowledge."

"He's tough, Plover," Baransky said. "That's another reason I hired him."

"You pay him out of your cut."

"What cut's that?" Baransky said. "You're keeping me as a slave."

"I meant your rations. Food. Water. You might get more when we're done. You split that with Slocum, too."

Slocum thought it was time to argue a bit more. To give in now would make Plover even more suspicious and likely to shoot him in the back. The argument over pay stretched for a minute until the foreman finally agreed to pay Slocum a dollar a day and not force Baransky to share rations.

"Better than what I expected," Slocum said.

Baransky let out a lungful of air he had been holding, fearful of the outcome. Any shooting that went on would likely see more than Slocum gunned down. He stepped closer so he could speak to Slocum without being overheard as they slid the crates of dynamite out and began lugging them toward the mineshaft.

"Why'd you bring her?"

"She's headstrong," Slocum said. "I didn't have much choice." He would let Melissa tell her pa how she had been mistreated by Trueheart and Sally and the rest of the scavengers.

Baransky nodded, looking glum.

"Did she get away?"

"I couldn't tell, but when I lifted the tarp, that gave her enough cover to get out of the wagon. It wasn't that far to the edge of a ditch on the far side of the road."

"Quit yammering, you two," Plover said.

"I must teach him the proper way of carrying the dynamite. You wouldn't want him to get careless and blow us all to kingdom come, would you?"

"Thought you said he knew what he was doing." Plover prodded Slocum with the rifle butt and sent him staggering into the mine.

"He knows how to use the explosive once it is planted. He's not used to carrying it like some beast of burden," Baransky said.

Slocum heard how lame that sounded and spoke up.

"I set the charges, I don't carry the dynamite."

"So you know how to do the blasting?" Plover shoved Slocum harder and got him walking down the narrow mineshaft.

Slocum wondered what use this shaft was since it brushed his broad shoulders. For a serious mine, tracks should have been laid for ore carts to move the tons of ore-bearing rock out to a smelter, where the precious gold could be squeezed out, ounce by precious ounce.

"I can do the blasting," Slocum said.

"Precision blasting?" Plover pressed.

Slocum looked ahead to get some idea what was going on, but Baransky was hidden in the darkness.

"I can drill, I can tamp, I can blast. What more do you need?" His mind raced. The only reason Baransky was still alive was his knowledge as a mining engineer.

"Can you do a mining engineer's job?"

Slocum tensed. A wrong answer meant somebody died. If he answered "no," then he was worthless. If he said "yes," Baransky was the likely victim. Plover didn't seem the kind to tolerate much waste—or surplus workers.

"I need somebody like Baransky to figure out where to blast. Once he does that, I can deliver as many pebbles from a wall as you like."

Plover fell silent. Slocum had given him reason to keep them both alive. For the time being.

They trooped on in the darkness until a faint light ahead showed. Baransky walked a little faster and so did Slocum, wanting to see something again other than blackness deeper than midnight.

They came into a large chamber lit by kerosene lamps placed around the fifty-foot circumference. What stopped Slocum was the ceiling. The light only penetrated a few yards and then was swallowed by darkness. A couple dozen men sat scattered around the large area, rifles leaning against the walls. They only glanced in Slocum and Baransky's direction before returning to their card games and other pursuits of bored men doing garrison duty. Three men held flea races on a hot griddle not ten feet from Slocum. Four others played dice. Others took their time to whet knifes or oil six-shooters. They were more an army than a ragtag bunch of scavengers.

For that was the way it seemed to Slocum. Trueheart had moved a small army into this cave. The only reason he could think was to keep them from getting into trouble in town—or getting drunk and letting the others know what Trueheart's plans were.

Slocum wished he knew. And then he realized he was going to find out soon enough. When he did, that likely meant he was expendable along with Baransky.

"This is a natural cave. Much of the mountainside is honeycombed with caves and tunnels." Clem Baransky pointed to the stalactites dangling from the roof. If any came loose, they would kill a man under tons of rock. "There are damned near a dozen naturally occurring tunnels needing only a bit of work to widen."

"Why bother?"

"Gold," Baransky said softly. "You hardly need to dig out ore. Scraping it off the walls is easy work and nuggets are everywhere. Trueheart took a wagon load out a couple weeks ago, but they've been working these tunnels for months. He's got close to another wagon filled with gold ready to take down the hill."

"Bypassing Almost There?"

"Goes on east, nobody in town any the wiser—either town."

"Why aren't the men working?"

"Something's up, something more important. He's only got a quarter of the men here he did when they were all scraping away at the rock. Don't know where they've gone but they've been out of here since before they brought me in to blast."

Slocum didn't ask about blasting near such a huge cavern. If Clem Baransky knew his job, he would decree that it was safe to blow open whatever passage Plover—Trueheart!—wanted. There had to be a mother lode Trueheart wanted revealed. But why would he get rid of three-quarters of his men? And where were they? Slocum hadn't gotten the feeling they were in Trueheart's personal town and they certainly weren't in Almost There.

"Keep going. Follow Doc. He'll tell you where we're gonna blast." Plover handed them carbide lamps and pointed to a tunnel leading straight into the mountain.

"It's quite a ways," Baransky said. "And there aren't any tunnels or chimneys for us to get lost in."

"How far's that?"

"More than a mile," he answered. "A lot more."

As they walked, Slocum began to struggle to breathe.

"Air's bad in here," Slocum said as his lungs began to strain.

"No ventilation. I want to set the charge, get away as far as I can, then blast."

"What's going on?" Slocum finally asked after a few more minutes of hiking. They were far enough from the large vaulted room that their words wouldn't carry.

"Listen. Do you hear it?"

"Water? An underground river?"

"You're right. Trueheart wants me to blow open a channel and release the water."

"Irrigation? That doesn't make sense," Slocum said.

"The man's a scavenger through and through. If my geology is right, once the rock wall we're blasting cracks, water will flood the lower part of the goldfields. We're more 'n halfway under the mountain, and the valley where the gold strikes occurred couldn't be much farther straight through the rock."

"So?" Slocum didn't understand. Then he did. "He wants to flood out the miners."

"Exactly," Baransky said. "The water will destroy their camps and mines and wash them out."

"Then he moves in and takes their claims."

"The mines will likely remain flooded. No, he is a

scavenger at heart. He wants to steal the gold that's already been smelted and whatever supplies aren't ruined. He's a carrion eater."

"Only this carrion bird doesn't mind killing hundreds of people to feast," Slocum said grimly. He knew where Trueheart had sent the bulk of his gang. They were likely in the goldfields now, waiting for disaster so they could take advantage, steal what they could, and then hightail it. An army of fifty scavengers could carry off a huge amount of gold and valuable mining supplies.

Slocum and Baransky came to the end of the tunnel. Through the wall ahead he heard the deep, throaty rumble of rushing water. Break this rocky dam and untold men would die, all so Trueheart could pick their carcasses clean. And Slocum couldn't see any way out of doing the scavenger's bidding. Either they set off the blast and hardworking miners died, or Plover killed them and had someone else do the detonation.

15

"If we blast through the wall and release the water, we'll drown," Slocum said, looking back down the pitch-black tunnel they had just traversed.

"I've thought of a way to string enough fuse so we can be well out of the mine when it blows," Baransky said. "That doesn't change the fact I'd be killing dozens—maybe hundreds—of miners."

"And all to steal their gold," Slocum said bitterly.

"I have studied this wall, and there's a chance this part of the tunnel wouldn't flood," Baransky went on. Slocum heard the note of excitement in the man's voice, as if he were a small child discovering a toy for the first time. "The shock would fracture the wall downward, and that would release the water only on the other side of the mountain. The pressure—"

"We'd still be responsible, even if we survived," Slocum said. He paused, his purple-white light from the carbide lamp falling on Baransky's face and giving it a curious pallid appearance.

"I know," the man said.

"What would Melissa and your son think of you killing so many?"

Baransky said nothing as he walked to the wall and pressed his hand against it. Then he leaned forward and placed his forehead against the cold rock. Slocum thought silent sobs shook the man but couldn't be certain.

"All I wanted was to earn enough for my wife's medical expenses. In Europe—"

"She's dead." Slocum saw no reason to edge into it.

Baransky swung about, eyes wide.

"What are you saying? She can't be dead. The doctors said she had months to live, maybe a year."

"Why do you think Melissa was in the wagon?"

"I don't know. I'm confused. So much is happening. It surprised me seeing her, but somehow it wasn't a shock. I mean, it was because I wasn't expecting to see her, but she was always headstrong. She argued against me coming so I thought she might have followed to persuade me to return."

"She and Stephen came to tell you your wife's dead," Slocum said, his words even harsher than before.

"Stephen, too? I can't believe he came. Or did he escort Melissa?"

"Seems the other way around to me."

"My children are here. I can't believe it."

Slocum remembered the letter Melissa had given him and reached into his coat pocket. The letter was water stained and in poor condition, but he handed it to Baransky. He opened the envelope and held the letter high in the carbide light beam. Slocum wasn't sure but he thought the man turned even paler. With shaking hands, Baransky tucked the letter into his own pocket.

"You have to prevent Trueheart from carrying through with his scheme."

"How?" Baransky turned away and muttered, "My children came after me. And she's dead. She's dead." He spun back, eyes hollow and haunted. "You're lying, Slocum. I don't know why. You'll do anything to keep me from carrying out Trueheart's orders. This letter is a fake."

"Was that Melissa in the wagon?"

"Why, yes, but—"

"That ought to be all you need to know. If Trueheart wipes out the mining camp, there's no reason to keep you around. Or your children."

"How'd she get into town to even climb into the wagon?"

Slocum spent a few minutes explaining how Melissa and her brother had hired him to find him. Baransky looked thunderstruck.

"I never meant for them to come with me. But Clara's dead. She shouldn't be. If I'd found the money earlier, if only—"

"There's no reason for Melissa and Stephen to stay with your wife's body. She's in a cemetery now. What did you expect them to do?"

"Stephen could have gotten a job and Melissa, well, she is a lovely girl. Marriage . . ." His voice trailed off.

"If you want to save them, you have to avoid setting off the dynamite," Slocum said.

"But the explosive is here. A lot of it. If we don't do it, Trueheart will find someone who can. The town must be full of prospectors who know something about detonations and bringing down rock in a mine safely. All he needed me for was the geological survey. Somehow, he had figured out for himself that he could loot the goldfields if the river was diverted from its subterranean channel."

"He's a clever one, I'll grant him that. But he doesn't care about the safety of anyone but himself. All he wants is the destruction so he can scavenge."

"What can we do, Slocum?"

There didn't seem to be much of an answer.

"Can you rig the dynamite to go off but not cause the damage Trueheart wants?"

"I don't think so. From all I can tell, any explosion against the rock face will cause the shock to pass down and through the river and blow out the far side of the mountain. It's not too far, I don't think, so the crack would spread fast and wide." Baransky put his hand against the cold wall again and shook his head. "This wall will surely be destroyed, too."

"Flooding the shaft all the way out through to the mouth of the mine," Slocum said. He thought hard on this. "Can you set the charge so that the water only comes this way?"

"Risk killing ourselves so those nameless, greedy miners can live! I won't do that! Not when my daughter is at risk from such a harebrained scheme!"

Slocum picked up a stick of dynamite and tossed it from hand to hand, as if getting the feel of it before hurling it.

"No, you can't do that. I know what you're thinking, Slocum. You want to toss a few sticks of dynamite into the chamber and kill Trueheart's men."

"That has occurred to me."

"We'd be trapped inside if the cavern roof collapsed. And it might."

"So we walk to the other side before lighting the dynamite and tossing it into the chamber. That would give us a straight run outside."

"Plover is no fool. He won't let either of us, much less the pair of us, cross the chamber. Trueheart's men are guards intended to keep me inside the mine."

Slocum touched his empty holster and knew that Plover would never have allowed him to keep his six-shooter under any circumstances. Even with a couple sticks of dynamite, it would be him against a small army.

"Why'd Trueheart put so many of his men into this cavern?"

Baransky shrugged, then said, "He's saving them. These are his elite fighters, the ones he culled from the dregs in town. I suspect he intends them to be the ones to get down the mountainside and guard the loot after the destruction."

"It'd take a week or more to cross Desolation Pass," Slocum said. Then he realized that it wouldn't matter how long it took. Trueheart controlled the western slope of the mountain so he could take his sweet time sending in these men to help the rest bring down the gold stolen from the mines.

"He has a self-financing operation," Baransky said. "He steals enough to keep the town going and provide supplies for his men. Selling equipment and mules he doesn't need down in Almost There provides money, but he keeps the food and anything else his scavengers need for this project."

"He doesn't even have to pay to have food or gear shipped halfway up Desolation Mountain," Slocum said. "The prospectors bring it to him, then he kills them."

"We can't get away," Baransky said.

"Damned right you can't get away," came Plover's angry voice. "I came to see how you were coming with the dynamite. You ain't started yet. You thinkin' on talkin' that rock wall down?"

Slocum reached for his six-gun, then checked himself when he saw movement in the darkness behind Plover. Even if it had rested in the cross-draw holster, he would have died trying to clear leather. At least two guards had come with him, maybe three. With him and Baransky at the end of the tunnel, backs against a rock wall, they'd fall easy victim to even one gunman since they had nowhere to run or take cover.

"You missed part of what Baransky said," Slocum explained. "We can't get away using so little dynamite. We need another crate, maybe two if this is going to work. Use too little and that might jinx the entire blast."

"Like hell. I'm no expert but I know bullshit when I hear it. We got all the dynamite you'd need. Which of you do I shoot?" Plover lifted his rifle and positioned it between

Slocum and Baransky. A simple twist one way or the other would select his target.

"I told you before, you need us both," Slocum said.

"People will die if we blow up this wall," Baransky said.

"Like I care."

"How long do you want the fuse to burn?" Slocum asked, a plan working its way into his brain. "You need to get all the men back there cleared out, or do you intend to kill them?"

This caused a stir among the three gunmen with Plover.

"He's just tryin' to drive a wedge between us, boys," Plover said loudly. "We'll all be out of the mountain 'fore the blast."

"Fifteen minutes? Twenty?"

"It's damned near a mile back to the chamber," Plover said. "If you run real hard, you can make it in ten minutes."

"Let's call it thirty minutes of fuse," Slocum bored on. "The air's mighty close in here. Hard to breathe."

"You have thirty feet of fuse?"

"More than enough," Slocum said.

"Set it for thirty. Me and the boys'll be back in an hour to make sure you've done the work."

Slocum and Baransky both threw up their arms to protect their faces when Plover fired his rifle. The report in the enclosed space was deafening and the slug bounced off a couple walls before spending itself in a side wall. Chunks of rock had splintered. Slocum touched his cheek where a razor-sharp piece had left a shallow cut.

"Just to get you workin'," Plover said, backing off. When he was far enough away, he spun, his men leading the way to the central chamber.

"What do we do now?" Baransky asked.

Slocum couldn't think of anything that would get them free, so he picked up a hammer and held it out to the mining engineer.

"You want to hold the chisel or swing the hammer?"

Slocum ended up using the ten-pound sledgehammer as Baransky positioned the bit at the spots he thought best. An hour later, they sank to the floor, covered in sweat and panting with effort. The lack of air made them both dizzy. For his part, Slocum found it hard to lift his arms after the hard work of using the hammer. The ring of steel on steel filled his ears and made thinking harder.

"We're going to die in here," Baransky said in a neutral tone, showing he was giving up. "Melissa and Stephen are safe, though. They have to be or this isn't worth it."

"Did you figure to get rich prospecting?" Slocum asked. He mopped his face with his sleeve, then ran his fingers over his empty holster. There had to be something he could do without needing a six-shooter.

"I wanted the money for the operation. In Europe," Baransky said in his dull voice. "We didn't have much since the last coal mine I worked for went out of business. The owner stole the money and lit out for California."

"You were on his trail?" Slocum perked up. This would show more determination in Baransky than he had seen.

"He died somewhere on the bank of the Red River. Got word of his body floating north into Canada, but I never saw it. But what does it matter if I ever found him? The money he owed me would be long spent."

"You really believed you'd get lucky?"

"Lucky? Mining's not about luck. Attention to details. Knowledge. Having a bit of intuition to know when to make a bigger gamble and when to back out. I'm a good engineer, not some wild-eyed prospector thinking he's the one who'll get rich when the rest around him starve."

Slocum looked at Baransky with new admiration. The man understood both the lure of mining and how to approach it for a better chance to make decent money.

"You didn't buy a treasure map or anything foolish like that?"

"I have a few photographs. Oh, not on me. In my luggage.

They *were* with my gear, but I don't have any notion what happened to them."

"Photographs?"

"Of the rock structure near the gold strike. If the locations are accurate, the prospectors are going away from the mother lode, not toward it. Such an opportunity! I could get enough for my wife's surgery."

"So you were broke?"

Slocum read the answer in the man's bleak expression.

"I had to do something, and there wasn't a job to be had near Philadelphia. Nowhere in Pennsylvania, in fact. Why not roll the dice and go for the big strike? Clara needed the operation. Poor, poor Clara."

"Poor you, especially since you think you can read where the gold is in the photographs," Slocum said dryly. Secret treasure map, photograph, it didn't matter. To Slocum they were one and the same, though the photos might be cheaper since they could always be tacked on the wall for decoration after they proved worthless.

"Didn't say I found gold there, only a better place to look. I'm an engineer, Slocum. The science I employ gives better odds but not a surefire find."

That made some sense. Hunting for blue dirt increased the odds of finding gold. Slocum had seen this work more than once for the old-timers while the greenhorns made their claims based on nothing more than a gut feeling and a dream.

"We've got the holes drilled," Slocum said. "Do we actually set the charges?"

"Plover will check. If we don't, we're goners."

Slocum got to his feet and began sliding sticks of dynamite into the three-foot-deep holes. It felt as if he'd stuck his head into a noose as he tamped the holes shut after crimping a blasting cap and attaching a length of black miner's fuse to each charge.

He exchanged a silent look with Baransky, then began splicing the black fuses sticking out of the rock wall to a single one that he unrolled back into the tunnel, walking toward the miles-distant rock chambers where Plover and the rest of Trueheart's gunmen waited.

16

"Hold it right there," came the cold words. Slocum looked over at Baransky, the intense carbide light turning his face into shadows and planes. He might have been a ghost he appeared so pale. In his gut Slocum worried that they'd both be real ghosts soon enough.

"You sure they set the charge right?"

Slocum turned his light past Plover, who blocked the way with his rifle leveled, and saw Trueheart. The man was dressed like a peacock, in a flashy green cutaway, purple vest, and striped pants. All that was missing was an appropriate hat but the tunnel ceiling was too low for that. Slocum had to walk hunched over to keep from banging his own head against rock. Trueheart matched his six-foot height and then some.

"It's properly planted," Slocum said when he saw that Baransky was too frightened to speak. He knew what Trueheart showing up now meant.

"Then light the fuse and let's run like hell."

"Boss, wait," Plover said. "We'd better head out first, then have them light the fuse when we're clear of the tunnels."

144

"Where's the fun in that? Race you!"

Slocum and Baransky exchanged looks. Trueheart was as crazy as he dressed. His plan matched his looks and behavior, but Slocum remembered the flood of equipment into his personal town and how the scavenger king had sent out bands of men to plunder along the trail over the pass. And then there was Sally and her whorehouse. He might act crazy, but he was a cold-blooded killer.

"You want it lit? Give him a head start," Slocum said, pointing at Baransky.

"All for one, one for all. Light the fuse." Trueheart's words came out cold and precise.

Slocum reached into his vest pocket, found his tin of lucifers, and lit one. It flared pale and almost invisible in the glare of the miner's lamps. He inclined his head slightly to warn Baransky, then he put the burning tip to the fuse. It sputtered for a moment, then the magnesium in the waxy black fuse flared.

"Yee haw!" cried Trueheart. He pounded down the tunnel, followed by Plover and two guards.

Slocum didn't know if he could run a full mile in the stuffy tunnel, but he had no choice unless he pinched off the fuse. To do that would bring Trueheart back—Trueheart and his murderous henchmen. While he ran, Slocum heard Baransky behind him, huffing and puffing, cursing now and then as he slipped, but keeping up. The run stretched to eternity, taking on an eerie quality in his carbide light, which bounced around as his head bobbed.

Then he burst into the huge cavern. Trueheart's men had already left. From the gasping and occasional curses, Slocum knew that Plover had fallen behind his boss by some distance.

"Can you make it the rest of the way?"

Slocum looked back down the tunnel in the direction of the charges they had planted, then knew he could never get back before the explosion. He had measured off somewhere between twenty and thirty feet of fuse. That gave twenty to thirty minutes before the detonation.

"Keep goin'," gasped Baransky. "I'll keep up."

Slocum got his arm around the man's shoulders and herded him forward. How long had it taken for them to get this far? He didn't know. He ought to have measured the fuse better, checked his watch to know the time of detonation.

"Ahead," panted Baransky. "I see the mouth of the—"

The explosion caused the ground to lift and buckle under their feet. Slocum crashed into the mining engineer and lay atop him as a rush of debris blasted above him. The shockwave stunned him, but he wondered why it wasn't hot gas searing his back.

As the dust began to fall from the roof, he realized a mile of tunnel had cooled it. Or was it something more?

"Water," he said. He dragged Baransky to his feet. "The tunnel's flooding!"

Gasping, they burst out into fresh air. They fell into the dirt in the middle of a ring of Trueheart's men. Slocum expected Trueheart to give the order to shoot them, but a look of awe on the man's face told how transfixed he was by the blast.

"Listen," Trueheart said so softly he could hardly be heard. "We have changed nature. We are like gods. *I* am a god!" He threw his arms into the air and spun in gaudy circles.

Indians protected their crazies, thinking they were touched by the gods. Seeing Trueheart and his victory dance caused Slocum to believe they were right.

"Water? The roar," Baransky got out. He stood with hands on his knees, bent over and still gasping for air. Outside the air was fresh, cold, invigorating. "It's going away?"

"The underground river is draining," Slocum said.

"How's that possible?"

"Let's find out. You two, ahead of us, and be quick about it." Trueheart motioned for Plover and another guard to prod the two back into the tunnel.

Slocum went willingly, because he was curious about what damage the dynamite had caused. Plover had a harder time forcing Clem Baransky back into the tunnel.

Stepping over rock and other debris that had been knocked loose from the ceiling and walls, Slocum reached the huge cavern. Some of the stalactites had tumbled from the ceiling, but the room was otherwise unaffected by the explosion. It took him longer to retrace his steps to where they had planted the dynamite because he didn't have the goad of being blown up to keep him running like a bat out of hell.

"Son of a bitch," Plover said fervently when they finally came to what had been the end of the tunnel. "I don't believe it."

Slocum edged forward and shined his light on a wet tunnel with only a trickle of water running down it.

"The explosion blew off the far side of the mountain," he said. "It drained the river."

"Into the goldfields," Baransky said. "It must have sent a huge wall of water erupting from the mountainside across the goldfields."

Plover said something to the gunman with him, then poked Slocum in the back. "You first. Let's go explore."

The empty waterway was worn smooth and slippery, but Slocum made his way for more than an hour along it. The last fifteen minutes inside the evacuated waterway he had strong wind in his face. When he reached the point where the shock of the explosion had blown a hole in the side of the mountain, he looked out and saw the devastation. Mine shacks had been washed away in the broad, saddle-shaped valley. Some mines lower on the side of the hill still gushed water and might for a long time. Anyone in those mines when the water broke free of its channel was a goner.

"We're right above the smelter," Baransky said. "That's the smelter—or what's left of it."

The water had poured through the structure and hit the

hot furnaces, which had erupted like volcanoes. Any workers nearby would have been killed outright. Slocum saw
where craters six feet deep had been blasted. Some still held
water like black stock ponds, but others had been eroded
away and spilled the contents still lower on the mountain
into the valley.

Slocum saw bodies strewn about the smelter as well as
glittering spots in the mud. Gold. Bars of gold smelted and
prepared for transport.

"We don't have to go clean over the pass to get here now.
This worked even better than the boss thought it would."
Plover lifted his rifle and sighted in on Slocum.

Slocum's hand twitched the slightest amount. He wasn't
going to allow Plover to cut him down without a fight, no
matter how futile. Before either man could make a move,
Trueheart's booming voice cut across the still landscape.

"Move on in, men. You know what to do. And Plover,
get them to hauling. Gold's heavy and we can use every
strong back we can find. It's not going to be long before the
survivors come looking for what we're taking."

Trueheart danced around a bit, his coat catching the first
rays of sunlight. The cloth had been woven with gold thread,
making him gleam like the gold scattered at their feet.

"Yes, sir, this is mighty fine. I'd thought to take a few
wagon loads of equipment, supplies, things left by the miners
that weren't too waterlogged. And gold. I never expected to
have a road opened up for me smack through the mountain.
Who needs cans of beans when we can all have bars of gold!"

Trueheart bent and pulled a bar from the sucking mud.
He wiped it off on his coat and held it aloft so the sunlight
glinted from its metallic edges. His laughter filled the valley.

"You heard him. Get to rooting around in the mud like
a hog. Don't want to leave a single bar of that there gold,"
Plover said.

"You going to help?" Slocum asked. His and Baransky's
execution had only been postponed. After they had moved

as much gold for Trueheart as they could, their reward wouldn't be golden but rather leaden.

"A good supervisor is worth two workers—at least the two of you," Plover said, an evil grin curling his lip. He motioned with the rifle for Slocum and Baransky to get to work.

It was past noon before Plover gave them a break. Slocum looked at the waist-high stack of gold bars. One of those could make him a rich man. The dozens he and Baransky had recovered from the flood plain would buy a fancy house on Russian Hill in San Francisco, entry to the Union Club every night, and all the Gran Monopole a man could swill.

Gunshots caused Baransky to perk up. He had been seated, back against the gold, head drooping from exhaustion.

"What's that? What's going on?"

"Trueheart's men are making sure the miners don't come back."

"Water's still gushing from the lower mines," Baransky said.

"Wouldn't matter to a man seeing a chance for wealth— or to jump a claim. Might even be some of the miners survived the flood, though I can't see how that's possible."

"The explosion must have cracked open the bottom of the channel and sent the river to a lower level. It'll flow for a long, long time. There's no way anybody is getting back to those mines."

"They'll try," Slocum said.

"Yes, I think you're right. I would have, if it meant my possible death weighed against gold enough for my wife's operation."

"Enough of that lollygaggin'," Plover said. "Get a sledge and start dragging some of this gold to the hole in the mountain."

"We're taking it all the way through to the other side?" Slocum asked.

"Start pulling, and we'll see." Plover's answer suggested

that they were safe enough if they worked to move the gold. When they reached the other side of the mountain miles off and through the empty river channel and mile of tunnel, they would become too much trouble to keep around.

Until then . . .

"I found a pallet," Baransky said, "that will be good for dragging along."

Slocum attached rope to the front of the wood and then helped Baransky load gold onto it until the slats began to crack.

"Can't load any more or the sledge'll break."

"So?" Plover didn't sound impressed.

"If we have to carry the gold one bar at a time, we'll be here for a month of Sundays."

The distant reports of rifles told Slocum how Trueheart's men were being challenged. There wouldn't be enough ammo in the world to keep an angry mob of miners at bay, especially if they realized how their hard-won gold was being stolen. Unless he read Trueheart wrong, Slocum thought the scavenger was more inclined to grab and run rather than stand and fight. He might not make off with as much gold, but his mentality was more like a crow stealing a suddenly shiny object than a beaver diligently building its dam.

"Get on with what you can," Plover said. He followed them a few paces as they struggled to pull the load through the muddy ground. Once when Slocum turned around to dig in his heels to yank the sledge onto a rocky stretch, he saw how Plover staggered along. Trueheart's henchman had picked up a gold bar for his own and was having an increasingly difficult time carrying it up the steep hill to the gaping mouth of the underground channel.

Trueheart stood just outside the empty channel, nodding as his men lugged gold into the mountainside.

"You are doing good work, you two. Especially you, Doc. Keep it up and you might find yourself with one of those gold bars."

Slocum held his tongue. The only way Baransky would be rewarded with a gold bar was if Trueheart smashed him over the head with it. It wasn't in a scavenger's makeup to share. He put his back to the work and got the sledge into the emptied riverbed. Slocum slipped and then found himself sailing along.

"The water's cutting friction," Baransky said.

"Easier pulling," Slocum agreed. He kept a sharp eye out for a way to escape. Many newly formed cracks along the floor showed where the river had been diverted. Somewhere ahead of them the main river had gone to a lower level, leaving this one empty. They reached the point where the wall had been breached before Slocum found an escape route for them.

Armed guards urged them into the tunnel. The going proved more difficult here, having to lug the gold over fallen rock, but eventually they reached the far side of the mountain, where a pair of wagons awaited.

Rather than go to Trueheart's town, Slocum wanted to take the branching road, the one to Almost There, and get the hell away. He knew it was more likely they would be shot out of hand now that they had done the work required of them.

"Trueheart's getting antsy," Plover called. "We're not movin' enough of the gold and them miners are gettin' guns."

"Strange how they'd figure all that gold they scratched out of the mountain with their fingernails and paid to have smelted into bars was theirs."

Slocum looked up to the driver of the far wagon. Mackley.

Mackley recognized him at the same instant.

"Well, what have we here? You'll use anybody to do your work for you, won't you, Plover?"

"Shut up." Plover prodded Slocum with his rifle. "Get the gold loaded in the wagon."

Slocum began lifting the heavy bars and piling them in the back of the wagon. When he realized he was the only one working, he stopped.

"What about him? Baransky?" Slocum turned but Plover struck him on the shoulder with his rifle butt. Slocum fell to his knee, pain filling his body. His muscles were burned out from moving the gold and felt weaker than a newborn kitten. He glared at Plover, who smiled crookedly at him.

"He's got other work to do."

"If the miners get too insistent on getting their gold back, Trueheart wants the tunnel blasted shut," Mackley said. "And it's my job to get this gold down the hill. Won't do to have it layin' about where the rightful owners might get it back."

"We're the rightful owners," Plover said, laughing. "We stole it fair and square!"

"You're going to steal it from the rest of your gang," Baransky called out.

"Get him back into the cave," Plover snapped. "Do it or I'll plug him and plant the dynamite myself."

Baransky was pushed and shoved back into the tunnel, screaming the entire way. Slocum tried to use the diversion to make an escape. Whether Baransky did it with this in mind or was only protesting his own fate, Slocum couldn't say, but he wasn't going to let it go to waste. He got his feet under him and launched himself so his shoulder hit Plover in the belly. The man's belt buckle cut into Slocum's numbed arm, but he didn't stop driving with his legs. Only when he hit a patch of sand covering rock did he slip and fall. This gave Plover time to recover.

Slocum looked up into the rifle muzzle.

"Good-bye, Slocum," Plover said. His finger tightened on the trigger.

"I still need him to load the gold," Mackley called. "When he's done, tie him up real good, toss him in the back of the wagon, and I'll take care of him at the bottom, after he's earned his keep. I can use him to unload down there."

"Why should I help when I know you're going to kill me anyway?" Slocum grated out. Needles of sensation danced along his arm. He rubbed circulation back. The deadness turned into outright pain. Careful flexing convinced him Plover hadn't broken his collarbone but otherwise he wasn't in good shape to fight.

"Here, catch," Plover said, tossing Slocum's Colt to Mackley. "It'd be good to shoot him with his own gun."

Slocum saw he had no choice other than to continue working. They were right. Every minute he worked was another minute he stayed alive. It took a while, but he finally loaded the gold into the wagon. The axles creaked and the wagon bed sagged under the heavy load. He spun, thinking to jump Plover, but the outlaw was too quick for him.

Plover kicked Slocum's feet out from under him. Once he knocked him onto his belly, Plover snared his wrists and expertly lashed them together. With a heave, he dumped him into the back of the wagon atop the gold. Slocum had to wiggle around to get the heavy metal bars out from under his ribs so he could breathe.

"Don't screw up, Mackley. I swear, you try anything and I'll kill you."

"You worry too much. Everything's goin' better 'n good, right? We're all rich men. I wouldn't do anything to risk my share."

Slocum almost called out to Plover to warn him of Mackley's plan, then bit back the words. Mackley didn't know Slocum had overheard. Somehow, he had to use that knowledge to his advantage.

The wagon shuddered and began rolling down the steep slope to the road leading into Almost There and away from Trueheart's hidden town. Mackley rode the brake, his left foot pressing hard into the wood lever. From the way the wagon threatened to overtake the six-mule team, he ought to have shoved a steel rod through the spokes and let the wagon slide down, wheels locked.

Slocum had to admire the way Mackley handled the wagon, though. He rounded the upper bend and started down toward the lower one, where Slocum knew he would let the wagon go tumbling over the edge.

"Yes, sir, this is my lucky day," Mackley said as he neared the sharp bend in the road. "I thought all I'd get was a bunch of stolen equipment, not a load of gold."

"Why not steal it all?" Slocum called. He worked to get his hands free, but Plover had been a cowboy at some time. His binding was as secure as any thrown around a calf's legs as it awaited branding.

"Trueheart is a man of some influence all over these parts. I'd have to kill him to make off with this much gold. No, better to steal more 'n my share and let him think it's lost. He has a fair amount of gold in that cave up there scratched off the cave walls, but this is beyond my wildest dreams. Trueheart's gonna get—"

The shot rang out over the creaking of the wagon and the grating of steel-clad wheel rims against rock. Mackley straightened, looked back at Slocum with a surprised expression, then reached down to his chest before toppling over in the driver's box.

With the strong hand gone from the reins, the mule team bolted and things went to hell fast. The tongue broke, the foot on the brake was dead, and the gold-laden wagon plunged over the edge of the road with Slocum in the back.

17

Slocum tried to curl up in a tight ball, but the force of the wagon leaving the road flung him outward. When he hit the ground, the air blasted from his lungs and sent him rolling downhill. He felt the cut of rock and thorn and then dropped into a ravine. Slocum lay flat on his back and stared up at the bright blue Idaho sky. His eyes went wide when the wagon arced over his head. As if it had been dipped in molasses, the wagon turned over in midair and then vanished from sight. The immense crash that followed made him cringe.

Then came only silence.

Slocum gasped for breath and finally fought to sit up. He tugged at the ropes binding his wrists, but the strands refused to budge and cut into his flesh until blood trickled.

"John! John! Where are you?"

He shook his head to clear it, tried to call out and discovered the words clogged up in his throat. He spat out blood, then gasped, "Melissa? Down here!"

Stones rattled nearby and then the sky was suddenly filled with a lovely angelic visage. Melissa stared down at

155

him, eyes wide in concern, then she dropped and kissed him
hard. He gasped and sputtered.

"Air, can't breathe," he finally got out.

He winced as she hugged him.

"Oh, John, you're alive. I didn't know what I was doing.
I . . . I shot him. I used a rifle I stole, and I shot him."

He rolled to his side and held out his bound hands as
much as he could in silent urging for her to free him. It
took Melissa a second to understand, then she set to work
with a vengeance, finally taking a sharp-edged piece of
flint from the ground and using it to saw painfully through
his bonds. He gasped in relief as his wrists finally popped
free.

"Oh, your poor hands. You're hurt." She kissed his hands
and wrists, then pulled back and made a face. She spat some
of the blood to the ground.

"Are you sure Mackley is dead?" he asked, accepting her
help in standing. He was shaky from the wreck and from
all the lifting and hauling he had done during the day. As
used to hard work as Slocum was, Trueheart had given him
chores that drained his strength to the point where he could
hardly stand.

"Let me help you up to the road," she said, her arm
around him. He held back for a moment, seeing how the
gold had scattered down the hill. The wagon had smashed
into splinters.

"Over there," he said, pointing.

"It's Mackley," she said in a choked voice. "You want to
make sure I killed him?"

"He's dead," Slocum said with certainty. Mackley's head
was twisted at a crazy angle. If the woman's bullet hadn't
killed him outright, the fall down the hill had.

"But—"

He pulled free and made his way to the corpse. Ants
already worked on Mackley's flesh, but Slocum cared less
about this than he did the gun thrust into the man's belt. He

yanked his Colt Navy free and held it up so it caught the sun's rays. It felt good settled once more in his holster. Slocum motioned for Melissa to begin climbing back to the road. Every step he took gave him renewed strength as he realized he was not only free, but had a chance to take revenge on Trueheart and his gang.

"What do we do now, John?"

Melissa looked at him as he made the final few feet of the slope and stumbled onto the road.

"Your pa's still a prisoner," he said. Slocum looked up the road, but dusk cast long shadows and the air turned chilly. "It won't do any good to go after him right away."

"We can't let him stay up there!"

"Trueheart has to come down this road."

"We can't let Trueheart kill him!"

Slocum nodded, understanding her concern. The instant Trueheart had no more use for Baransky, the man was a goner. He hadn't thought it through, and she was right. Trueheart wouldn't come down the road, surrounded by his gang—and with Clem Baransky. Slocum wasn't sure Trueheart would even leave his hideout with many of his men. Setting them against each other was more in keeping with the way Trueheart operated.

He wasn't a leader—he was a scavenger, and he reveled in picking over the remains left by others.

"You still have the rifle you used to shoot Mackley?"

"There. Over there," she said. She had propped it against a rock before sliding down the hillside to help him. Melissa hefted the rifle and looked determined. "We're going after Papa, aren't we, John?"

"Yeah."

"Oh, John, I knew I could count on you."

"You saved me. Mackley would have killed me after we got down the hill."

"Don't think you owe me, John. I can save Papa on my own," she said defiantly.

Slocum explained what had happened and how Baransky was likely to remain alive if Trueheart needed him.

"He's a smart man. He'll draw out the work setting the charges as long as he can, but Trueheart isn't stupid either. Eventually he will have to blow up the tunnel and won't care if it is done right."

"The entire mountain might come down," Melissa said. "Papa explained that to me repeatedly when he worked in the coal mines. The geology has to be studied and every possible outcome weighed."

"Trueheart won't care," Slocum said, "but your pa might take it into his head to blow everything up and take Trueheart with it."

She started to speak, then clamped her mouth shut. She put her head down and started walking faster. The conclusion Slocum had already reached finally occurred to her. Baransky might kill himself if he could take Trueheart and his men with him in one huge blast.

Slocum wished he still had the carbide lamp to light the way. The darkness was close to absolute, heavy clouds hiding the sliver of rising moon and blanket of stars. They began to stumble as the night deepened, then came heavy drops of rain pelting against his hat.

"We could push on," Slocum said. "It'd be better if we found cover and waited out the storm."

"I'm mighty tired," she said reluctantly. "Where can we go?"

"There's got to be a cave around somewhere," he said. He put his arm around her shoulders and guided her off the road, up a slope, and to a spot blacker than the surrounding terrain.

"A cave! How'd you see it, John?"

"By contrast with the rock around it," he said, herding Melissa inside just as the sky opened and a deluge caused raindrops to dance a foot or more off the rock. He sank to the dusty floor and watched the rain move closer to the cave

mouth. He took off his hat and held it in a small river draining from above to capture enough water to wash off the dirt
he had accumulated during his blasting and freighting for
Trueheart.

"Let me help, John. You are a sight."

Her fingers slipped under his collar and pulled his coat
away. He dropped his gun belt where it wouldn't get wet and
stood, letting her strip off his vest and shirt. The water
splashing onto his bare back from the rain sent a shiver
through him—or was it the rain? Melissa's fingers worked
across his chest and down to unbutton his jeans. As she
worked on his fly, he kicked free of his boots.

"Time for a bath," he said, standing naked before her.

"Want company?"

In answer, he reached out and unbuttoned her blouse and
cast it aside. It took a bit more work, but he got her naked
to the waist. Her perfect breasts gleamed dully in the dark.
He worked more by feel than sight, taking the pair into his
palms so he could squeeze down until she moaned and
stepped forward, crushing them into his palms.

"So nice," she cooed. "More. I want more."

"Greedy bitch," he said as he kissed her cheek and
worked back to her ear. His tongue flicked out, lightly traced
around the lobe, and dipped deeper in promise of what more
would come.

"You haven't seen anything yet, mister!"

She finally stripped off her skirt and pressed hard against
him. They stepped back a pace so the water cascaded over
them. Slocum gasped at the cold but relished the slickness
of her skin moving sensually against his, the stimulation of
the rain, the vibrant feel of her young body, the gusts of
wind that blew across his nakedness.

"More, I want more."

He slipped his hand between them, past the deep valley
of her tits, across her belly, farther, and then curled around
and entered her with his middle finger. She tensed. He began

working it around within her as she became slipperier, and not just with the rainwater. Her hips moved in rhythm as she lifted one slim leg and hooked it around his back to pull herself even closer.

Slocum had to abandon the finger in her hot core when she grasped his hardness and insistently tugged it toward her crotch. He wasn't going to complain. She stood on tiptoe, positioned herself, tensed the leg around his back, then plunged downward. They both gasped with the sudden intrusion.

Surrounded by clinging, moist, hot female, Slocum supported her by grabbing a double handful of ass flesh. They danced out into the rain and let the water pour over them. For what stretched to an eternity, Slocum contentedly reveled in the feel of her around him, deep within her, arms around his neck, supporting her weight and letting the rain fall.

When she began tensing and relaxing her inner muscles, he found it impossible to simply stand. Fires banked within his loins began to flare. The heat burned downward toward the end of his manhood, but he fought it back.

The ordeal he had been through and the emphatic movement of her hips robbed him of both balance and strength. Slowly sinking to the ground, still out in the driving rain, he laid her back.

She looked up at him, eyes aglow. Darkness hid much of her body, but Slocum felt skin move slickly under his fingers, rubbery nubs at the crests of her breasts, the heaving of her chest, the way her knees drew up on either side of his body to open wantonly for him.

"Hard, John, I want it hard."

That's how he delivered it. The lovemaking took on animal intensity until they both cried out. Slocum rammed forward, trying to split her in half. She responded by shoving her hips down against his to take him even deeper inside. The speed built and then neither could hold back any longer. They clung to one another and then sank down, spent.

"It's even better when we don't have an audience," he said.

"I never noticed. Either then or now."

Slocum laughed, kissed her, then began running his hands over her sleek body to remove the mud they had accumulated with their lovemaking. She returned the favor, and clean, they returned to the cave.

Both began shivering from the cold.

"We need a fire," she said.

"Mine's gone out. For a while."

"Only a little while, I hope." Melissa fit into the circle of his arms and shared bodily warmth until they both dried enough to put on their dirty clothing.

"I wish we could wash these filthy rags," she said, giving a shimmy to settle her blouse. "We were clean, and now I feel dirty."

"How dirty?"

"Oh, you." She punched at him playfully. He caught her wrist and pulled her close. She didn't resist his kisses.

After a while they settled down, not speaking, watching the rain fall outside their snug cave.

Slocum drifted off to sleep, only to snap awake when he realized the sun was coming up over the horizon. Melissa still slept in the circle of his arms. He shook her gently.

"We'd better move. Trueheart's not going to wait."

"Papa," she moaned softly, then came fully awake. "Oh, dear, we haven't let him—"

"We need to get your pa away from him," Slocum said. The chances of Baransky being alive had diminished with the rain. Trueheart might not be able to get down the steep road, but he had no reason to keep his prisoner alive either.

Slocum stood, strapped on his gun belt, and saw that Melissa clutched the rifle she had used to shoot Mackley as if she faced Trueheart.

He looked out at the steep hillside leading down to the road. New gullies had been cut into the ground by the fierce rainstorm. Slocum took one down to the road, sliding more than walking. Melissa joined him.

"How far is the mine?"

"Not too far," Slocum said. He studied the road, its turns, and decided they had come closer than he'd believed possible the night before. As they walked, he kept an eye out for Trueheart and his men. They would be on the move anytime now.

"I hear wagons," Slocum said. "They'll be coming down the mountain any second."

"There," Melissa said, pointing. "We can shoot them from there!"

Slocum doubted that shooting it out with the gang would be possible. Better to concentrate on freeing her father, and if Clement Baransky was already dead, letting Trueheart and his scavengers go their way. Justice wouldn't be served but at least Melissa—and Slocum—would be alive.

They hiked up to the spot, but Slocum didn't like it as a vantage. The field of fire was too limited.

"Higher," he said. "We need to get up where we have a better view of the road and what Trueheart's doing."

Melissa grimly climbed, every muscle tense. She kept up with Slocum as he explored to find the right spot. She ran into him when he stopped suddenly.

"What is it?" she asked.

Slocum took a few seconds to understand what he was seeing.

"That's your brother, and he's going to shoot Trueheart."

Stephen Baransky was going to bring the entire gang down on him, ending all their chances for living to see another sunrise.

18

"Stephen!" Melissa cried. Slocum clapped a hand over her mouth. She struggled, then subsided when the wagon passed below them, slewing in the mud and making enough noise to drown out her outcry.

Slocum scooped up a handful of pebbles and heaved them with all his might. They pelted Stephen, causing him to roll onto his back and swing his rifle around. For a moment he didn't see who had thrown the stones, then he spotted Slocum. The expression of stark hatred on his face made Slocum think he was going to fire.

"Melissa! What are you doing here?"

The young man's question took Slocum by surprise. He had seen his sister and thought she'd tossed the rocks. As Slocum moved, Stephen spotted him for the first time. Again the rifle swayed, as if to fire, but this time it centered on Slocum.

"Put that down, you little fool," Melissa said hotly. She dropped to her knees beside her brother and forced the rifle away.

Slocum didn't relax as he made his way down the rocky

incline. He kept Stephen squarely in view. For the world, it had seemed he was going to gun down his own sister—after he had recognized her. He hadn't seen Slocum until a second or two later.

"You disappeared. I had to track these . . . vultures . . . myself."

"Papa is their prisoner. If you'd shot at Trueheart and missed, he would have killed Papa. We're trying to get him free."

Slocum shoved Stephen flat when another wagon made its way past below them on the road. He recognized Atkins driving and wanted to turn Stephen loose but common sense made him hold back. They had no chance in a shoot-out with Trueheart and his men.

"Have you see him? Your pa?" Slocum demanded.

The answer was slow in coming. Stephen finally shook his head and muttered, "No."

Slocum wondered why he was lying when he wasn't any good at it. And why would he lie about this at all?

"You stay here. I'll go after your pa."

"No!"

Slocum looked hard at the young man. Was he finally growing a pair?

"Stay here with your sister. I won't be long."

Slocum slid farther down the incline, then began moving so that midsize rocks shielded him from the road. A third wagon passed on its way down to the town below. Whatever Trueheart had promised those in his own little town, they were being robbed blind. The gold-laden wagon that Mackley had driven was only the beginning of the caravan. While he couldn't tell what rode in these wagon beds, from the way the wood sagged and the axles creaked, a considerable amount more of gold had been stolen from the miners on the far side of the mountain.

Slocum worked his way farther along, then ducked when he saw Trueheart sitting as proud as a peacock in the driver's box of a fourth wagon. His fingers tapped the butt of his six-shooter, but Slocum knew he would never win the war if he opened fire. Trueheart might be dead, but so would he. The scavenger leader had his usual three bodyguards riding in the back, all of them holding their rifles and looking far too alert to allow anyone to get away with even a single quick shot.

After the wagon rounded the sharp bend in the road, Slocum skidded the rest of the way into the mud and began slogging toward the mine opening. He saw a few horses tethered nearby, warning him that some of the scavengers remained. It told him nothing about Baransky or if he still lived.

He paused in the mouth of the tunnel, not wanting to venture into the depths of the mountain again. Faint sounds from the large cavern echoed out to him.

". . . when we gonna get rid of him?"

"The boss said we could play with him awhile, if we wanted."

Slocum recognized Plover's voice. His heart beat faster with expectation because the snippet of conversation he'd heard meant Baransky wasn't dead. Not yet.

"I want to get the hell out of here. I'm sick of bein' surrounded by nothin' but rock. Don't know how them miners stand it."

"You're getting paid a pretty penny," Plover said. "Buck up, man. We're all rich men."

"Five wagons of gold." The wistfulness in the voice caused Slocum to draw his six-shooter and begin a silent stalk into the tunnel. "Each of us gets ten bars. We're rich."

"What are you going to do with yours?" Plover asked.

Slocum crept closer.

"Whores. Whiskey. Maybe buy myself a spread, but not in this godforsaken country. Too many mountains. There's got to be a piece of land in Nebraska wanting to get parted by my plow."

"You're not the farming kind. You'd miss the excitement."

"Like hell."

"There comes Doc," warned Plover. "Over there, in case he tries anything."

"What can he do?"

Slocum moved to a spot just beyond the cavern to see both men bathed in the brilliant purple-white light of carbide lanterns. Plover had his pistol out, and his partner held a rifle.

"The fuse is lit," Baransky said, stepping into the light. He held up four sticks of dynamite taped together, a long black fuse sizzling with eye-popping fury in the darkness. "You try to kill me, you'll never get to the dynamite in time and it goes off and brings down the roof."

"You'd kill yourself," Plover said. A bit of anxiety tinged his words, but he wasn't outright afraid. He thought he held the upper hand.

"One way or the other, I'll be dead. I blasted down the roof back there. Twice I brought it down because the miners were tunneling through after you."

"Should have counted how many sticks of dynamite you were given and how many you used," Plover said. "Guess it's a mite late for such foresight."

"If you both get over to one side and let me out of the tunnel, I won't kill you."

"Now that's plumb stupid, Doc. We let you run and you're *sure* to blow the tunnel and seal us in."

"What're you sayin', Plover?" The other outlaw's voice trembled. "We got ourselves a Mexican standoff?"

"Looks to be. None of us is goin' to get out of here alive 'less we declare a truce."

Slocum saw Plover nod to his partner. Plover moved away to draw Baransky's attention. Stepping out, Slocum squinted against the bright light, lifted his six-shooter, and fired in a smooth motion. The man with the rifle grunted, dropped his rifle, and pressed both hands against his chest.

He looked up dully and said, "I'm hit, Plover. I been hit." He sat down, then slumped over, dead.

Plover wasn't standing still. He got off a shot at Baransky, then spun and fired fast and wild at Slocum. Driven to the ground, Slocum had no chance to finish the chore he had started.

"I'll blow you all up!" shrieked Baransky. "Give up or I swear I'll blow us all up!"

"Get down," Slocum shouted. "You're making yourself into a target. And put out the fuse!"

For a moment it seemed as if Baransky was paralyzed. He stared at the dynamite in his hand, as if he had no idea what it was. Then he plucked the fuse out and threw it from him as if he had inadvertently picked up a rattlesnake.

Slocum rose enough to take a shot at Plover. The scavenger managed to take a couple shots at Baransky, but they missed by a country mile. The sounds of the slugs bouncing off rock and whistling about lit a fire under Baransky, driving him back in the direction of the blasting he had done.

"You still in one piece?" Slocum called out the question more to occupy Plover than to get an answer from Baransky. The mining engineer had moved right sprightly, so he wasn't hurt. The shock of everything happening around him was more likely to slow him than a bullet through a leg or arm.

"You're like a bad penny, Slocum. You keep comin' on back, over and over, where you ain't wanted."

Slocum tried to get a good shot at Plover, but the stalagmites provided too much cover. He dropped back and scooted along on his belly, hunting for a better place to attack.

"That you, Slocum? You came back for me?"

"Me and your daughter and son."

"I can't believe it. They risked their lives for me?"

Slocum wanted Baransky to keep talking. Nothing distracted Plover, however. He knew Baransky didn't have a weapon now that the fuse had been pulled from the bundle of dynamite. That left only Slocum as a danger.

Part of Plover's hat poked over a rock. Slocum knew better than to let the man draw his fire. He waited, patience his major virtue now. When the hat didn't move, Slocum knew Plover had propped it up and was moving to get the drop on him. A slow smile came to his lips. Only one course was possible.

Turning in the direction where Plover had to appear, Slocum waited. And waited. When the light suddenly died in the cavern, Slocum fired. Plover had snuffed out the carbide light in an attempt to confuse Slocum. If he had continued to watch the hat for movement, he would have fallen easy prey.

Slocum's six-shooter showed foot-long tongues of orange flame as he fired three more times. The first shot was dead center where he thought Plover would be in the dark. The other two shots bracketed the first, one left and the other right, to be sure he hadn't guessed wrong.

A new muzzle flash showed, this one aimed downward. The bullet hit rock and sent up a shower of debris.

"Can you get to the other carbide lantern?" Slocum called. "I think I nailed him, but I don't know. I have to see to be sure."

Slithering sounds allowed Slocum to follow Baransky's progress. When the light poked up and gave enough illumination, he knew the man had reached the fallen carbide light.

"Shine it toward my voice."

Slocum shifted his aim when he saw a dark form slumped over a rock. He started to squeeze off another round, just to be sure, but Plover didn't move a muscle. Baransky moved closer with the light, and Slocum saw his barrage had proven deadly. His first shot had struck Plover in the left arm. One of his others had hit the man in the cheek. He approached, indicated how Baransky should use the light, and saw that another of his bullets had drilled through the man's other cheek and into his head. The slug had exited out the back of Plover's head, leaving a hole the size of a silver dollar.

"Good riddance," Baransky said.

Slocum looked at him.

"What happened? In the tunnel?"

"Trueheart had me set dynamite but wouldn't let me set it off. Too many of his men already in the goldfield hadn't gotten through to this side yet."

"More likely, they all had gold, and he was too greedy to abandon them—and it."

"Probably," Baransky said. "I finally set off a small charge but hadn't calculated it right. It brought down a small piece of roof in the old water channel."

"The miners dug through it?"

"Fast. They were like moles. Never heard men work so fast. Trueheart had me set off another blast to trap them."

"You miscalculated that on purpose?" Slocum saw a different answer on the engineer's face.

"I . . . no. I tried to blow them up. Something went wrong with the dynamite, and it sputtered rather than exploded. They kept coming. The third blast got them all."

"Trueheart would have killed you if you hadn't. How'd you come to have that bundle of dynamite?"

"Trueheart thought I'd died in the last blast, but Plover was smarter. He knew I was coming. He stayed back with his partner to kill me, but I found more dynamite. I wasn't joshing them. I would have blown us all up. I would have!"

"Let's get the hell out of here." Slocum closed his eyes for a moment and thought he heard scraping sounds. Or maybe it was the tommyknockers, the creatures that inhabited mines that warned miners of danger.

They stepped out into clean air. The rain has washed it clean of dust and left the day bright as a shiny new copper penny.

"I can't believe they would have come for me, not after everything."

"Melissa's a hellion," Slocum said. "Surprised me a mite that Stephen was willing to kill Trueheart to avenge you. He thought you were dead."

"Amazing how life can change a man. Stephen was always a lazy good-for-nothing. When we had the money, it wasn't so bad, but when my wife's medicine soaked up more and more of our money—" Baransky shook his head. "Stephen wouldn't get a job. Insisted on spending what little we had."

"Melissa like that, too?"

Baransky laughed at Slocum's question. "She is a frisky colt, always jumping about and racing around. But there's not a lazy bone in her body."

"I know that," Slocum said, remembering how they had explored each other's bodies. He was particularly fond of the flesh on her bones.

"How's that?"

"Mount up. We can get back down the road to where I left them."

"What of Trueheart?"

Slocum explained how the wagons, laden with gold, had left, and he finished with his suggestion that Trueheart be allowed to go on his way.

"No! I'll find the law. I'll see him swing from the gallows!"

"Fine words, but there's no marshal here. Don't know how far off the county seat is, and I doubt the sheriff would be much interested if Trueheart offered him some of that gold."

"He killed men. He stole. Worse, he robbed miners of their dreams! He has to be brought to justice!"

"Let's find him first, then decide," Slocum said. He pretty well had made his decision to let Trueheart go his way. The man had a small army and a mountain of gold. That

combination bought a lot of forgiveness—or forgetfulness—
in this part of the world.

As much as he would have liked to see Trueheart in jail,
Slocum faced the truth. It wasn't likely to happen.

"I'll make it my life's work. He kidnapped Melissa. What
he did to her is a terrible crime!"

"He'll come to a bad end eventually. Go back to Philadelphia with your son and daughter. Make a new life and
forget Trueheart."

Baransky rode in silence until Slocum raised his hand to
stop his descent along the road.

"I left them here," Slocum said.

"Melissa likely took justice into her own hands."

"That was what Stephen wanted, not her." Slocum dismounted and studied the trail left in the mud. The ground
held a silent message that required a considerable amount
of work on Slocum's part to decipher. He swung back into
the saddle.

"What is it, Slocum?"

The words burned Slocum's tongue, but he had to tell
Baransky the truth.

"Trueheart has taken both Melissa and Stephen prisoner."

"What happened?" Baransky choked out.

Slocum didn't know, but he had to find out. For Melissa's
sake. For his own peace of mind. Too many times he had
let down members of the Baransky family. But not this time.
Not now.

19

As he rode, Slocum kept looking over the edge of the road, fearing that he would see two bodies cast down the slope and angry when he didn't. Why had Trueheart taken both Melissa and Stephen prisoner? Melissa was easily enough explained. She was a beautiful woman, and Trueheart might want her for his own before either killing her or sending her back to Sally's cathouse. But Stephen Baransky was another matter.

"He might be following Trueheart to free her," Clem Baransky said, breaking Slocum's concentration.

"How's he following? He was on foot." Even as Slocum spoke, he realized that might not be true. He and Melissa had come upon her brother as he lay in ambush. He might have hidden a mule or horse off the road. It had not been a matter to consider at the time, not with Stephen intent on shooting down Trueheart.

"Stephen and I never got along well, but one thing I can say about him, he's not a dull boy. Always thinking."

Slocum would have said "scheming" but he didn't know Stephen as well as his pa. His gut feeling remained, though.

He didn't much care for Stephen or his attitude toward his sister or anything else.

"I keep looking down the road to see if I can spot the wagons, but they made better time than I would have thought," Slocum said.

"Where's this road go? I was brought up from Trueheart's town."

"It feeds into the main road just east of Almost There. Trueheart must have stumbled on it because I can't see him cutting a road on his own."

"He has a small army doing whatever he wants," Baransky said. "I found that out every time they took me to his town. For all I know, he owns all the businesses there. He certainly had dozens of miners working to scrabble out gold for months until he hit on the idea of flooding the goldfields. So he might have built it just for his own purposes."

Slocum doubted that. Trueheart was a scavenger. He stole things others dropped. If it was necessary, he would kill so they'd drop items. In many ways he wasn't even an honest thief. A road agent had no problem shoving a gun under his victim's nose, but Trueheart worked in the shadows, darting in as a sneak thief. Slocum wondered if the grandiose plot to flood the goldfields and steal whatever floated up was Trueheart's idea or if one of his henchmen had come up with it.

"When did he discover the underground river?"

"What?" Baransky jerked around to face Slocum. "I don't know. Plover was proud as punch about the idea of drowning the miners. He had a beef with somebody there."

In the end it hardly mattered whether it was Trueheart's seeking carrion in the watery ruin created or Plover wanting revenge. Men had died, their claims ruined, and Trueheart had made off with more gold than he could ever have imagined.

They rode past the spot where Mackley had been shot. Slocum trotted close to the edge of the narrow road and tried to find the gold that had been spilled. Only a few pieces of the wagon were visible. A detached, battered wagon wheel was the most prominent evidence that someone had left the road in a bad way.

"What are we going to do?" Baransky asked. "How can two of us go against Trueheart and all his men?"

"I've got an idea," Slocum said, taking one last glimpse over the side. He hated to give up the gold that had been in Mackley's wagon, but a trade for Melissa and Stephen might be the only way. Trueheart had tasted gold. He would never leave well enough alone and had to succumb to the fever that had infected all the prospectors and miners. There could never be enough gold in any man's possession.

They reached the junction of the mountain road with the main road going into Almost There. Slocum rode a few yards in each direction before seeing that Trueheart had avoided the town in favor of driving due east.

"He's not taking chances. He's hightailing it out of the territory," Slocum said. For all his failings, Trueheart showed good sense at times. This was one of them. Four wagons creaking under their golden load should never be exposed to the avaricious nature of the men outfitting themselves to crawl over Desolation Pass and risk their lives for a nugget or two. The prospectors might be honest enough, but given the chance for real wealth, not many would stay that way. The lure of sudden riches had brought them to Desolation Mountain.

Killing an outlaw or two to become wealthy beyond their golden dreams would be an easy price to pay.

"How long before we overtake them?" Baransky asked after they had trotted along for a half hour. "They can't be that far ahead of us."

"They aren't," Slocum said. "There's a bend in the road not a quarter mile away." He pointed. "They're camped just beyond it."

"Camped long?" Baransky choked voice carried the real

question. Had Trueheart and his gang been there long enough to do unspeakable things to Melissa?

Slocum hoped Baransky never found out about how she had been used for long days in the brothel.

"Let me go ahead and scout. We've got to approach this careful-like or Trueheart will start shooting. We won't come out on top of any gunfight."

"What can we offer him for Melissa that he would want?"

"Leave that to me," Slocum said. He felt a reluctance to burden Baransky with too much information, not that the man could do anything about the spilled gold from Mackley's shipment. Explaining what had happened and how his daughter had shot and killed a man might be more than Baransky wanted to hear.

"Don't take too long."

The simple statement hung in the air as a warning. Baransky felt the pressure of time on him, maybe more than Slocum did.

Slocum dismounted and tossed the reins to Baransky before setting off on foot to scout the camp. The scent of burning pine came to his nose just a bit before coffee and frying meat. He worked his way toward the side of the road, then down into a field and around through a wooded area that blocked anyone ahead from getting a good view of the road behind.

He cursed the blackberry bushes and their thorns, then silently endured the tiny scratches as he got closer. Pulled off the road in a small clearing were two wagons. What had become of the other two didn't matter since this cut Trueheart's gang in half. There were still too many scavengers for him to deal with alone. Slocum watched for a few minutes and finally spotted Trueheart.

The man had flopped on a blanket under a wagon. When he stood, he put on a top hat and strutted to the fire. Slocum drew his six-gun and took careful aim, then lowered his pistol. He had to know if Melissa was still alive, and if so, was she with Trueheart or had he sent her along with the missing wagons.

He stepped out into plain sight and called, "I've got a deal for you, Trueheart!"

A half-dozen men sprang up, rifles ready.

"I've got Mackley's wagon and the gold in it."

"Is that you, Slocum? I declare, you have more lives than a cat."

"I'm nowhere near going through nine lives," Slocum said. "You've got an opportunity to get even richer."

"A golden opportunity? Is that what you're offering?"

"Mackley's gold for Melissa Baransky."

"Who? Oh, the girl. Baransky? Can it be that she's related to Doc? That explains a great deal." Trueheart did a dance around the fire. Slocum couldn't tell if it was supposed to be a war dance or if the man was just crazy.

"There was a powerful lot of gold. She's worth trading."

"What became of Mackley? Oh, never mind. I don't care to know. He must be dead. Good riddance. I always thought he was something of a sneak thief, looking to rob me when I wasn't looking. But I'm always watching. Always watching and thinking."

"The girl, Trueheart. Do you have her?"

"What if I don't? Is there anything I can trade for Mackley's gold?"

"John, I'm here. Be careful!"

Melissa's words came from beneath the wagon. But Slocum didn't need the warning. He dropped into as crouch as a rifle slug tore past his head. He fired twice. His aim proved better than Trueheart's gunman.

"Don't go trying to ambush me, Trueheart. I'm not alone."

"Do tell? Is her daddy with you? This might be a situation where we can hold a family reunion." Trueheart stopped his cavorting about and stood squarely facing Slocum. "Where do you fit into the Baransky family, Slocum? You got designs on the little lady?"

"I've got gold, you've got the girl. Do we swap?" Slocum moved a bit more to his right to put a tree trunk behind him. He heard small movement in the woods and worried that another of Trueheart's men had sneaked from their camp and circled around. Worse, it might be Clem Baransky coming to poke his nose in at the worst possible time.

"How do I know you've got squat, Slocum?"

"Where's Mackley?"

"He ought to be halfway to Thompson Falls by now."

"He's dead, and I have the gold."

"You value her that much? But why not? Sally said you performed in a real spectacular fashion to get her out of the whorehouse. What else would you do for her, Slocum? What else? Why don't you show me and my boys what else you'd do for her?"

Slocum knew Trueheart was goading him. There were too many of the scavengers for him to ever hope to stand off if real shooting started. Worse, Slocum was aware that he carried only four rounds in his Colt now. He couldn't reload without Trueheart giving the word to attack him.

"John!"

He saw Melissa on her feet by the wagon. She had slipped out of whatever ropes held her ankles but her hands remained tied behind her back. She twisted about, then dashed away.

Slocum saw instantly that she had made a bad mistake. If she had just run, she might have reached the edge of the woods. Trueheart was moving even as she called out. He caught her around the waist and swung her feet up off the ground.

"Got her, Slocum. I got her, and I'm keeping her."

"The gold, Trueheart. You harm her and you'll never get the gold Mackley had."

"I'm rich now, Slocum. Can a man spend that much more?"

"Ask your gang. They'd all like five more bars of gold

apiece. Or maybe it's ten. There was a powerful big load of gold that came down the mountainside with Mackley."

Slocum started walking steadily toward Trueheart. He kept his hand at his side so the six-shooter wasn't obvious, but the scavenger knew he had it. All of Trueheart's men did, too. But he hardly seemed a threat walking as he did.

"He'll kill us both, John. Save yourself!" Melissa struggled in the circle of Trueheart's arm securely around her waist. Kick as she might, he was too strong for her.

"Go on, John. Save yourself," mocked Trueheart.

"The gold. Your men think it's a good deal trading the girl for more gold."

"I don't care what they think!" Trueheart glanced to the side when one man came up, rifle pointed at his boss.

"We want more gold," the outlaw said. "You want the girl, you pay for her out of your own cut."

"You—"

Trueheart tried to face his insubordinate man but ended up staggering. Melissa kicked him hard in the knee, almost dropping him to the ground. She jerked free.

"Down!" Slocum bellowed as he lifted his six-shooter.

Whether she obeyed or simply fell didn't matter. Slocum fired twice. A third time. One of the slugs hit Trueheart and he fell forward, writhing on the ground and crying out in agony.

Melissa got her feet under her again and rocketed toward Slocum. He had a single round left but couldn't figure out which of the scavengers to shoot.

He looked down at his gun foolishly when a shot spun around the outlaw who had confronted Trueheart. Then all the outlaws opened fire. Slocum found himself bowled over as Melissa crashed into him. Again going to the ground saved both of them. Rifle fire from the woods drove the outlaws to cover.

"Come on," Slocum urged, then he picked up the girl and put her on her feet. There wasn't time to free her hands, so they ran bent over, him helping to keep her from falling until they found cover behind a tree.

Slocum whirled and fired his last shot in the direction of the wagons, then worked to reload. He looked up to see Clem Baransky come from deeper in the woods. Smoke curled from the rifle muzzle.

"Thanks for saving my bacon," Slocum said. He turned and threw some lead in the general direction of the wagons. For every shot he fired, the outlaws returned five.

"Is he dead? Trueheart?"

"Can't say," Slocum admitted, "but he was in a bad way."

"What are we going to do?" Melissa asked.

"We're going to run for it," Slocum said. "We can't out-gun them."

"No! They must be punished. Brought to justice. I've got to know if Trueheart is dead!"

"What about Stephen?" Slocum asked. "Was he tied up with you?"

"Stephen?" Melissa spat out the name. "He was respon-sible for Trueheart catching me. I don't know where he is."

"Doesn't much matter," Slocum said, seeing Trueheart's men finally beginning to come together and make an attack plan. "You two stay back. Shoot if I tell you." He handed Melissa his six-shooter, then stood and went to a spot where he could duck for cover fast but was visible to the outlaws.

Slocum shouted, "We're about evenly matched in fire-power. I want a truce."

"What kind of truce?" Whoever answered wasn't Trueheart.

"We don't want to end up dead. We don't even want the gold. You get in your wagons and drive away. Otherwise, we're going to be shooting each other till there's nobody left."

"You'd let us go scot-free?"

"With the gold." Slocum heard Baransky hiss like a snake behind him. He motioned for the man to stay quiet.

"What about Trueheart?"

"What about him? He's dead. Take his body with you or leave it behind for the buzzards. We don't care."

"We don't know if he's dead."

"Then leave him for us and you drive off. Time's getting short. and my posse's thinking about trying to take you all."

"We're goin'. With the gold."

Slocum edged back into the forest and put a tree between him and the outlaws. He held out his arm to keep Baransky from rushing out to confront the scavengers. They hitched up the wagons and within fifteen minutes rolled away. The campfire still burned. Otherwise, there was no trace that anyone had been in the clearing.

"Now we go," Slocum said, after the second wagon had rumbled out of sight.

"I have to know," Baransky said. "I have to know if that son of a bitch is dead."

Slocum took his six-shooter back from Melissa.

"Let's see," he said softly.

He and Melissa followed Clem Baransky to the campfire and beyond to where a body lay stretched out on the ground. Slocum knew it was Trueheart from the gaudy clothing, but he didn't know if the man was alive.

He aimed for the head as Baransky kicked Trueheart hard in the ribs. No one living could have taken such a blow without reacting.

"He's dead," Baransky said. "The son of a bitch is dead!" He fired his rifle into Trueheart's back, then kicked him again.

Slocum understood Baransky's rage. Trueheart had died, but maybe he ought to have lingered awhile longer to appreciate his fate.

"I—" Baransky never got further. A shot from where they had been in the forest caught him in the chest and knocked him back so he tripped over Trueheart's body.

Slocum spun, thinking the gang had decided the deal was too good to be true.

"Drop it, Slocum. I ought to kill you outright, but I won't since you did me the favor of bringing both of them here." Stephen Baransky held his rifle snugged to his shoulder.

"Stephen, you—"

"Shut up, Melly. Just *shut up*! I'm sick of you and him telling me what a wastrel I am. He spent all our money on Ma when it was obvious she wasn't going to make it. It was kinder to kill her outright and put her out of her misery."

"Stephen," Melissa said. "What are you saying?"

Slocum knew. He went cold inside.

"She was hurting, Melly. She was hurting bad. I helped her. I *helped* her!"

"Why'd you come out here after your pa?" Slocum asked. "Why not let him prospect for gold?"

"You don't know anything. Grandpa Nate's in a sorry way. When he dies real soon now, he'd have left everything to him." Stephen jabbed the gun in Clem Baransky's direction. "He'd find a way to waste the money. My money! My inheritance!"

"Grandpa Nate's not sick," Melissa said. "He's in better shape than Papa. He—oh!"

"You were planning on killing your own grandfather," Slocum said. "Why not? You already killed your ma."

"It's my money. By rights, mine."

"So you are going to kill your own pa so you'll inherit?" Slocum almost wished he was dealing with Trueheart again. The scavenger didn't kill blood relatives.

"We can share, Melly."

"Go to hell."

"I thought you'd say that. I'll tell them you and Pa were killed by road agents. They'll believe me. Grandpa Nate will be so distraught over the death of his last son and his only granddaughter that he dies of a heart attack. They'll believe it."

"And you'll get his property? Is it a lot?" Slocum asked.

"He owns a shipping company worth a fortune. I'll be a shipping magnate and turn it into a worldwide business. I can do it!"

"You're going to murder your entire family?" Slocum asked.

"What did they ever give me? Nothing. Yeah, I'm going to!" Stephen turned to shoot Slocum, but Clem Baransky moaned and stirred, pulling his son's attention back to him.

Before Slocum could close the distance between him and Stephen, a shot came from a few feet away. Stephen grunted, yanked the trigger on the rifle, and sent a round high into the night sky. Then he toppled backward and hit the ground hard.

Melissa stood, both hands holding Slocum's Colt. She stepped forward and started to shoot her brother again.

Slocum took the pistol from her before she could duplicate her pa's punishment of Trueheart. He held her wrist to keep her from advancing to kick the downed man.

"He's dead," Slocum said softly. "Your pa's still alive. See to him."

Melissa wrenched free of his grip and clung to her father, sobbing bitterly. Slocum prodded Stephen, but his sister's aim had been deadly. He picked up the fallen rifle and went to where father and daughter clung to each other, sobbing.

"I'll see you into town," he said.

Melissa looked up at him, her eyes wild.

"Go, John. Just go. We'll be all right. Get out of here."

He started to ask if she wanted him to bury Stephen, then thought better of it. Slocum made his way back to his horse and mounted.

On the road, he considered directions, then a slow smile came to his face. There was only one place to go. He put his heels to the horse's flanks and started back to where Mackley had driven the gold-laden wagon over the side of the road. He might not be able to carry much of the gold, but a couple bars riding in his saddlebags would be decent payment for all he had gone through.

And with the gold, he could ride anywhere, if it was far away from Desolation Mountain and the Baranskys.

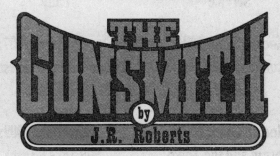

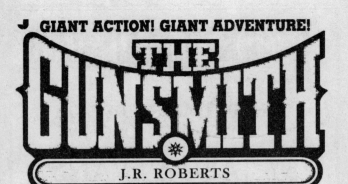

J GIANT ACTION! GIANT ADVENTURE!

THE GUNSMITH

J.R. ROBERTS

GIANT-SIZED ADVENTURE FROM
AVENGING ANGEL LONGARM.

BY TABOR EVANS

2006 Giant Edition:

LONGARM AND THE
OUTLAW EMPRESS

2007 Giant Edition:

LONGARM AND
THE GOLDEN EAGLE
SHOOT-OUT

2008 Giant Edition:

LONGARM AND THE
VALLEY OF SKULLS

2009 Giant Edition:

LONGARM AND THE
LONE STAR TRACKDOWN

2010 Giant Edition:

LONGARM AND THE
RAILROAD WAR

penguin.com/actionwesterns